PRAISE FOR NICHOLAS HASLUCK'S EARLIER NOVELS

Nicholas Hasluck has been a significant and engaging novelist on the Australian literary scene for half a century now. His achievements from *Quarantine* and *The Bellarmine Jug* to *Dismissal* and *The Bradshaw Case* are well attested. His books are not only a good read but they have something to say.

Michael Wilding, *Quadrant*

* * *

Quarantine is a tense, subtle and exciting novel set in Egypt, when a beat-up old ship is inexplicably detained at a small deserted port on the Suez Canal … I have not been as impressed or moved by a first novel for almost as long as I can remember. I think we are welcoming a truly important writer.

Martin Seymour-Smith, *The Financial Times* (London)

* * *

Nicholas Hasluck tells a lively story while sustaining an undertone of growing desperation.

Jeffery Burke, *New York Times Book Review*

* * *

Quarantine introduced the combination of intrigue, dark humour and fable that have become characteristic of Hasluck's style … *The Bellarmine Jug* explores the roots of Australian identity on both personal and social levels using techniques from the spy thriller that probes each layer of truth to reveal alternative realities … Hasluck continues to develop his highly individual vein of intelligent and inventive fiction.

Louis James, *Contemporary Novelists* (UK)

An infinity of mirrors is a definition of espionage. *The Bellarmine Jug* is compelling reading. I finished it at a sitting, ever anxious to know what would happen next.

Humphrey McQueen, *Sydney Morning Herald*

* * *

Hasluck discusses notions of justice, expediency and integrity with wit and compassion. *The Bellarmine Jug* could be read as an academic thriller or as an examination of civilisation and culture.

Gabrielle Lord, *The National Times*

* * *

The Country Without Music is a triumph, a combination of vividness and subtlety that confirms his position as one of the very few major novelists writing in Australia today ... A drama is played out that symbolises much of what may be seen as an essentially Australian problem: life in a society that has somehow lost its positive traditions and identity. The work rises above being mere satire by the skill with which its genuine human characters are presented.

Hal Colebatch, *Arts Review*

* * *

A Grain of Truth shows how a novel built out of legal practice, post-colonialism, politics and anecdotage can be informative, provocative, free from the constraints of the purely documentary, and offering powerful entertainment at the same time.

Andrew Peek, *Australian Book Review*

* * *

In *Dismissal* Hasluck has turned his hand to the political thriller. His well-structured set piece hinges on the Whitlam dismissal, one of the handful of events in Australian history capable of stirring genuine emotion and debate.

Andrew Croome, *The Weekend Australian*

* * *

Hasluck's absorbing novel, *Our Man K,* is enlivened by a sense of uncertainty, of the shadowy paradoxical implications of grand gestures, allegiances and beliefs … He has understood that for us in our time Egon Kisch may be a better subject of fiction than of political analysis.

Andrew Riemer, *Quadrant*

* * *

Rooms in the City from prize-winning novelist and former Chair of the Literature Board Nicholas Hasluck, is elegant period espionage fiction set in Greece during WWI. It evokes a web of intrigue that may pose a threat to the top-secret withdrawal from Gallipoli. The narrative crafts a tense shadow-world with a cloying atmosphere.

Cameron Woodhead, *Sydney Morning Herald*

* * *

The Bradshaw Case illuminates some of the complexities that have plagued native title law in Australia. In doing so it explores recurring themes in Hasluck's literary work: the tension between the world of law and facts, and that of justice and truth.

Zoe Bush, *Brief*

* * *

Hasluck is in the mainstream of satire, but descends more directly perhaps from Huxley, Orwell and more recently from Kingsley Amis and Keith Waterhouse.

Greg Sheridan, *Quadrant*

* * *

The three novelists considered here are veterans … While working as a lawyer in Perth Nicholas Hasluck wrote poetry, short stories and novels of which *Quarantine* was the first. *The Bradshaw Case* is the 13th. … These three veterans – Callinan, Aitkin and Hasluck – have made signal contributions to Australian public life. They can also be saluted for the achievements in fiction that are no doubt as dear to them.

Peter Pierce, *The Weekend Australian*

Other Books by Nicholas Hasluck

Novels
Quarantine
The Blue Guitar
The Hand That Feeds You
The Bellarmine Jug
Truant State
The Country Without Music
The Blosseville File
A Grain of Truth
Our Man K
Arbella's Baby
Dismissal
Rooms in the City
The Bradshaw Case

Short Stories
The Hat on the Letter O
Wobbling the Whiteboard

Essays and Memoirs
Collage
Offcuts from a Legal Literary Life
Light That Time Has Made (ed.)
The Chance of Politics (ed.)
The Legal Labyrinth
Somewhere in the Atlas
Legal Limits
Jigsaw: Law and Literature
Art in Law
Beyond the Equator: A Memoir
Rollo's Way
Bench and Book

Poetry
Anchor and Other Poems
Chinese Journey
A Dream Divided

CHE'S LAST EMBRACE

NICHOLAS HASLUCK

ARCADIA

© 2022 Nicholas Hasluck

First published 2022 by Arcadia
the general books' imprint of
Australian Scholarly Publishing Pty Ltd
7 Lt Lothian St North, North Melbourne, Victoria 3051
Tel: 61+3+9329 6963 / Fax: 61+3+9329 5452
Email: enquiry@scholarly.info / Web: www.scholarly.info

ALL RIGHT RESERVED

ISBN 978-1-922669-81-0

Cover design Lucia Sankovic

To
my companions
in South America

It is possible that this may be the finish. I don't seek it, but if it should be so, I send you a last embrace.
From Che Guevara's farewell letter to his parents

* * *

I see Che as a moral giant who grows with each passing day, whose image, strength, and influence have multiplied throughout the earth.
Fidel Castro at the Che Guevara Memorial, Cuba, 1997

* * *

Life is other than what one writes.
André Breton

1

MARVIC LAREDO'S ARTICLE

To face the camera. To be seen as we were and as we wished to be. That was what some of us wanted from the photographer. It was probably what he was looking for too, a glimpse of the here and now to be carried into the future. A memorable image, like the snapshot of our leader after the Cuban revolution. A click of the shutter, and there he was: the beret, the dark searching eyes and resolute expression. *Che Guevara!* The heroic freedom fighter! Could something like that be done for us?

To me, this seemed far-fetched. We had no claim to fame. We were just a bunch of *reclutas*. Recruits from all over the place. And as our leader didn't seem to be with us on this terrace at San Andrés, there to say a few words to those he had chosen for his next campaign, it struck me that a snapshot of our group might not mean much in times to come. Without Che up front we were nothing. Just a bunch of mavericks. Unless we managed to win through to what it was all about. Che's dream of a widespread revolution across South America.

Now, it seems, in the light of what happened later, we have to speak well of the photo taken that day. Each of us, as the photographer said while pushing us into place, *una cara de circunstancias:* with a face of circumstance. Facing whatever. You must look the part. Hence the brave look on so many faces. But what is one to think of it all? Such a strange photo. So many unreal events marking the start of Che's final venture.

Our venture, if what we did can be called that, has been given a second life by our leader's heroic image. So be it. Whatever we did was certainly a far cry from the original plan. *Con el tiempo va a ir mejor,* as Che would often say on the campaign trail: *things will go better in time.* It was the sort of thing he liked to say, even at the very end. When there was nothing much left to be said.

The place where we trained for the task ahead, like the photo on the terrace, had to be kept well-hidden. And so, even today, 30 years after our final battle in the ravines of the Chaco region, on this special day set aside to honour Ernesto 'Che' Guevara, I have to be careful. Say the right things. It might seem out of place to mention the secretive mood surrounding the early phase of our venture. But how else can I explain what happened? The worries, the stumbling blocks, the betrayals. I have to use it, the word always drilled into us. *Prudencia.* The need for caution. It affected everything we did.

Che's dream for South America is now so well-known it's in the history books. His plan to spread new ideas. Ferment a radical mood. Forge links to *campesinos*, farmers, and indigenous leaders. The training phase in Cuba with Fidel's backing. The building up of a multi-national force. Until, at last, *guerra de guerrillas,* guerrilla warfare! In the rural areas at first, then attacks in the cities. His tactics have been outlined at length by various know-alls. They do it with hindsight, of course, the lucky bastards, not knowing how it was for the *reclutas* pushed into place for a photo shoot. For those who were there at the beginning.

The size, the vast scale of Che's dream. This worried some of us, especially the day the photo was taken. The plans being discussed by Che and his Cuban friends seemed not only far-fetched but steps that could be fatal. *Si. Nada en absoluto.* No end to it. The faces staring bravely at the camera might reappear in the future. But where would they be seen, these pictures? In the pages of a revered album? Or in some dilapidated courthouse in the wilds, used as evidence against us, before facing a firing squad?

A multi-national force fitted the plan for widespread revolution, certainly. And it seemed appropriate that the recruits milling about on the terrace while the photographer set up his tripod had been drawn from all over the place. Countries subjected to imperial oppression, such as Cuba, Argentina, Guatemala, Bolivia, Peru, and even Paraguay, my birthplace. But the patchwork quality of the battle-dress worn by some of those around me pointed to a different and more worrying *facción* in the group.

Their khaki trousers, grubby tunics and battered forage caps were an eyesore. Everything about these men was a blunt reminder that some of those being herded into the photographer's frame had formed part of Che's ill-fated guerrilla force in the Congo. They were fully aware that revolutionary dreams aren't easily accomplished. Some of them, still haunted by the trauma of their defeat, less than a year before, may well have been thinking more of the past than the future. *Desamparados*, the homeless, perhaps. Lost souls gaping at the camera. Wondering what might happen to them now in another far place.

One thing I know for sure. For me to say too much about the doubts in the air as Che's new venture got underway is not so good. Things like that may unsettle some readers. That was made plain by the editors who twisted my arm to write my article. *Truth-telling, please.* But what they meant was: *don't write to please yourself or times to come. Write what people want to hear. What they deserve.* Here and now in Cuba, 30 years after the final battle, on this day set aside to bury Che Guevara, some tributes will be published, including yours, if all goes well.

It's a reburial, in fact, in a special tomb named in Che's honour. His body brought back to Cuba at last, to where he truly belongs and as the world expects. *So write what you know, but say it well. No frills.*

I know what is wanted and have said I will do my best. Come up with words that will serve the desired purpose. But where to begin? When I think back to the start, having promised to stay on the narrow path, it's not so easy. On the terrace perhaps, the day the photo was taken to mark the start of our venture, it sounds fine. But my training as a journalist tells me to add details, to look at the picture as a whole. I have to give some weight at least not only to the brave faces but also to the underlying mood amongst us. The feeling of uncertainty. The worries about secrecy; the routes taken to reach our camp at San Andrés. The masking of our names and identities along the way. The general unease.

The mood was there in the graffiti, on a wall in an *inodoro* at the camp, just inside the door. Someone had chalked up: *Soy rebelde. Y que? I'm a rebel. So what?* The apprehensive mood can also be seen in what followed: our startled response to an uproar after the photo was taken.

The group had begun to break up. Then, without warning, came an angry shout. *Hola!* A voice up front, but from where? Then we saw him. A grey-haired fellow who had been standing in the front row, older than most of us, unshaven, with a large paunch above his belt, was raising a fist. He shouted again. *Hola!* With one big stride upwards he found a place for himself on a parapet wall at the edge of the terrace. He lowered his fist and put his hands on his hips. *Reclutas,* he called out. *Reclutas.* Loudly. As if giving an order. But as we drew near, not quite knowing what to do, his hand became a fist again. He shouted louder. *No me voy,* he declared. *I'm not leaving.* He flapped at one of the Peruvians who had turned away. 'Listen to me! And listen hard!'

Then he thumped his chest, as if to identify himself, and shouted his name: *Adolpho Mena-Gonzalez!* Once more, in an angry tone. *Me llamo Senor Adolpho Mena-Gonzalez!*

This name meant nothing to me. Never heard it before. For a moment, by his age and the look of him, I wondered whether he owned the property, the buildings and cane fields around our encampment. A landlord with some complaint? But no, nothing he said seemed to fit this impression. So there he was, up there on the parapet in front of us, a silhouette against the sun behind him, a balding, middle-aged fellow of medium height. Thick horn-rimmed glasses. Speaking rapidly, jabbing a finger at us now, like an irate teacher picking on troublemakers at the back of the class.

Guerra de guerrillas, he shouted. 'Guerilla warfare is violence and the use of force. All other tactics can be thrown out the window. *A deber de todo revolucionaro es hacer la revolucion.*' He said this several times. '*A revolutionary's duty is to make the revolution.*' And more: '*Remember why you're here. Don't forget who you are. Are you dogs of war? Or scurvy dogs? An unruly pack of shit-eaters? Why waste a photo if you're only jackals? Only hyenas?*'

On he went, back and forth on the low wall. Shouting out things that made us stare.

It all seemed mad. We could scarcely take in what was being thrown at us: a wild rant about the fiery souls of revolutionaries. The way to win. How to crush the old regime. How to overthrow the tyrant. How it all depended on networks in the cities, guerrilla bands in the countryside recruiting locals to the cause. These bands, he shouted, would grow. They would double in size. They would use their networks to infiltrate the cities. To share power with the uneducated masses would be a waste of time. That would come later. The role of the guerrilla bands was to destroy the state by seizing power for themselves. But a multi-national force of that kind had to be worthy of such a triumph, as had happened in Cuba.

Power was there for the taking. Power was there for those who pushed ahead and grabbed it.

This didn't sound like socialism to me. Nothing like the ideas I had been brought up with, the workers first and foremost. But I didn't have time to work out what was what, for suddenly I heard my name being shouted out. 'Marvic Blas Laredo!' Then he called my name again, a couple of times, and louder. *Laredo! Laredo!* I don't quite know why – partly in panic I suppose – I held up my hand. To show I was there. '*Si Senor. Me llamo Marvic Blas Laredo.*' But this led merely to another shout from the mad old teacher on the wall. This time with his finger pointing straight at me. 'Laredo from Paraguay!' he shouted. 'The boy soldier! *El Australiano.*'

My boyhood days were over, but I couldn't argue. Not with him. For now he was telling the throng, loud and clear, what most of them already knew. That I was a Paraguayan. Descended from the Australians who had settled there in the 1890s. Idealists who went to form a new society. Brimful of radical ideas. This was the sort of man we needed now.

Fortunately, he didn't repeat the 'boy soldier' tag. My flicker of fame in the Chaco war between Paraguay and Bolivia had long since come and gone. I had no wish to revive it, for Bolivia's defeat at the hands of its smaller neighbour had always been a sore point, and there were several Bolivians in our group.

The mad old speaker on the wall must have seen the risk in this: to harp on about the Chaco war would annoy the Bolivians. So he changed tack. Left me alone, and moved back to his main point: the multi-national make up of our force. *Paraguay, Chile, Peru.* Wherever we came from, we shared a revolutionary dream. And not so long ago, he reminded us, a group like us had sought to seize power in Argentina. This was the new way of doing things. *No podria ir mejor.* Power grabbed by a group who know best.

What he said made me uneasy – and others too. I sensed the restive mood around me, a memory perhaps of the carnage wrought by the Chaco war, the damage done to both countries. Paraguay was generally seen as the victor, but the conflict had brought ruin in its wake. Was that what he wanted?

Surely not. All that fruitless debris in the depths of the Chaco region. It hadn't brought about what I wanted. I quit Paraguay while the war was still going on and crossed the border into Argentina. There I picked up work as a newspaper cadet in Buenos Aires. I worked on various left-wing papers, and years went by. I debated Marxism all over the place, but I never heard a plan to grab power of the kind being laid before us now.

As we watched, still bewildered by the words being hurled at us by the loudmouth on the wall, the bespectacled figure striding up and down, waving his arms about like a sailor cursing the reefs around him, another more extraordinary thing happened. He grabbed his glasses, stuck them in the top pocket of his jacket and began tearing at his clothing. He tore apart the buttons on his shirtfront and reached in, laughing almost fiendishly as he did so, and plucked out a grubby towel from somewhere above his belt which he flung over his shoulder. Then another. He aimed it at a recruit standing just below him, a Congo veteran perhaps, a bearded soldier who seemed to be laughing too, as if enjoying the same joke.

The way they kept grinning at each other, as the speaker went on stripping off, set me thinking. They might be friends, or at the very least former comrades.

The man on the wall kicked off his battered mud-caked boots. Hopping on each foot in turn, he struggled out of his old grey baggy pants to reveal khaki ones underneath. Finally, like a clown in some circus act preparing for a final bow in a burst of applause, still chortling, he pulled off a kind of skull-cap. This had given him the look of a balding man. Now he held it up and waved it about.

'The man you've been listening to,' the speaker declared, 'was Adolpho Mena-Gonzalez. He still exists. He, or someone like him, with some other name perhaps, will be leaving Cuba in a few months' time. By a roundabout route, through Vienna, Prague or Frankfurt, he will enter South America as a Uruguayan businessman. Well-behaved, without attracting attention.'

Hola! He waved the wig again, his little flag, the last remnant of his costume, and tossed it to the Congo veteran in the front row. Then he stood up straight. 'The man before you now,' he declared, 'is Che Guevara.' He dug into the pocket of his trousers and produced a black beret. Slowly and carefully he fitted this to his head.

Yes, it was Che! I was amazed. I was struck dumb by what we had just witnessed. Our leader, who had seemed so strangely absent when the photo was taken, nowhere to be seen while the photographer began packing up his tripod and camera case, had in fact been with us throughout. In disguise, then suddenly emerging. And with us now, as if by magic. We were in the presence of Che Guevara, the real man, with his resolute gaze and commanding presence. When the fellow at the front of our group, the one who had been laughing loudly as the disguise came off, began to applaud, sharing the joke, the piece of theatre, the rest of us began clapping too.

Entonces! We clapped and clapped and stamped our feet. It was the moment for such things. Such an overwhelming surprise. I felt such joy. *Che Guevara!* Our legendary leader had been with us all the time. He was with us now. He would always be with us – whatever happened. I couldn't be sure to what extent he meant the wild things he had been saying. Just part of his act perhaps, a piece of stagecraft to draw us in, to make us think, before surprising us. But that scarcely seemed to matter. I felt as most of those around me did: he had thrown down a challenge. We were now alive, alert, fulfilled. The mood had changed completely.

Che surveyed us calmly. There was something kindly, a father's look, about the way he did this. A moment later, as if drawing together everything that he had said, he added, speaking now in a firm and considered voice, what I took to be the true expression of what he had in mind: 'It is not always necessary to wait until all the conditions for revolution exist. The process of rebellion will create them.'

These words were clearly designed to quell any doubts as to whether the poor of South America were truly ready for widespread revolution, a vast uprising of the kind being planned. 'Steps will be taken to set the stage,' he went on. 'What has to be done will be done.'

But first we had to learn from what we had just seen. Make use of it. The need for subterfuge. Secrecy. Mastery of disguise. The importance of passwords. Crossing borders. The setting up of urban supportive networks brought with it the need to cover one's tracks. Create false identities, fake passports. He tapped his chest. 'Ernesto Che Guevara de la Serra,' he said. 'Your *commandante* when the bullets are flying.' He tapped his chest again and winked. 'Adolpho Mena-Gonzalez at the border, or in the back streets. A dreary old businessman from Uruguay. And what is he elsewhere? At a desk with a pen in his hand? Or here in our training camp? Or at our base in the jungle?' Che quickly mentioned two other aliases, ticking them off with an invisible pen. 'I can be Ramon. Or Mongo.'

He pointed to a swarthy, thick-set fellow at the group's edge. 'Eliseo Reyes Roderiguez. Well-known to some of you. But goes also by Rolando. He was with me when we crushed Batista.'

Then, with scarcely a pause for breath, Che singled out a Cuban of African descent, a fellow in a tattered battle-jacket who had been with us earlier in the day, to explain the layout of the camp. 'Harry Villegas Tamayo,' he declared. 'Better known in the cane fields and back streets of Havana as Pombo. Or occasionally Carlos. He was with me in the Congo and never faltered. Like many of you, he will be with us to the very end.'

Our leader took a few steps along the wall and turned to face us again, shoulders back, a finger in the air, poised to make a new point. 'Subterfuge includes the use of propaganda. Slogans for the *campesinos* and masses in the countryside. We will spread unrest, with handbills and broadcasts put together by our networks in the cities. We will shape opinions. Educate the masses. And for that we must draw upon our many skills.'

He stood still, to point at me again. 'Marvic Laredo. A veteran of the Chaco war and now a writer from Buenos Aires. As I once was myself. We can use your skills, if Paraguay, or even Bolivia, becomes the first flashpoint, the place to ignite our continental revolution. Laredo and his friends will go in early – in his case, simply as himself. Just a reporter from Buenos Aires, looking for a job. Some cover story on the surface. But soon he will be hard at work after dark, in secret. He and others like him will seed the ground with articles and interviews. His aim? To highlight the flaws and failures of the current regime.'

His finger was pointed at me again. 'How will he do it? By hints and asides. The incompetence of the Bolivian generals in the Chaco war. That can be suggested by mentioning a few of General Kundt's defeats. And this, of course, is the beauty of subterfuge. A smoothly-written article purports to be simply a factual piece about the history of a war, so that its author avoids being prosecuted for sedition. But everything he says will remind people of what's wrong with Bolivia's leaders. They can be presented as puppets or marionettes, influenced by foreign training, dancing to the tune of their imperial masters: *Estados Unidos de America,* and its rotten rent-boy, the CIA.'

He waved a cautionary finger. 'But none of this means Bolivia is necessarily to be our starting point. It has many disaffected people in the rural areas, true. *Campesinos* and *indigenas originarios* waiting to fall in behind a guerrilla band. But we need more. The support of Communist allies will be vital. And Argentina is still the main goal. Remember the planning behind the recent Argentinian uprising led by Jorge Masetti, our dead comrade and dear friend. He loved the masses and knew we had to fight for them. But remember the old Spanish proverb: *Hay amores que matan. There are loves that kill.* His fate is a reminder to us all. From first steps to the final attack, guerrilla tactics depend on secrecy. So keep a close watch on what you say and do. No loose lips. These are the basic lessons of your training.'

Everything Che said that day was correct. And his passionate tone made us long for action. *Muchas gracias.* It was more than enough to convince me that our group was special and could be trusted. We were truly *compañeros.* When he finally stepped down from the wall, and the group began breaking up, my sense of security was heightened by what happened next.

With the strongly-built Pombo by his side, Che came up and tapped me on the shoulder. *Amigo.* He began chatting to me in a friendly tone, returning to what he had said about the way my background as a journalist could be put to use. Up close, intimate, eye to eye, he began giving greater detail of what had to be done. Everything was laid out in a confidential manner. He pushed his beret back from his brow. His silent but clearly sympathetic side-kick, the taciturn Pombo, kept nodding in agreement.

Our encounter lasted only a few minutes. It was almost as if we were three fellow writers sharing opinions about some recent contretemps in the literary world: another quarrel at Café Tortoni, or a fierce debate at some other venue in Buenos Aires. Trenchant comments about the latest censorship ruling perhaps.

But not so. Our talk was far more important. Casually, but firmly, he underlined his point about using apparently innocent articles for propaganda. He began to speak about the skilful use of particular words and phrases. 'In a tightly-controlled society, people become accustomed to reading between the lines. Looking for coded signals. A calm style can be used to mask an argument for radical change. A piece about folklore or some missing artefact can be used to suggest that an entire culture is in need of reform. It has to be rebuilt in a certain way. Words and phrases, well-used, can lead to everyone thinking in a similar way. The way we want them to think.'

I was overawed by his magnetic presence, I soon found myself nodding enthusiastically at everything he said. I had read a number of his articles on the Cuban revolution and the role of *guerra de guerrillas* in modern times. And his travel diaries. It flattered me to be treated simply as a fellow wordsmith, although I knew, in my heart of hearts, that he was in a class of his own. Only he could perfect the subtle strategy he was laying out. I sensed immediately that beneath his good-humoured and apparently reasonable tone lay some brutal ideas and a ruthless plan of action. He would seize power whatever it cost.

I didn't know then that the three of us on the terrace at San Andrés, chatting in this friendly but purposeful way, were in fact destined to share a literary connection. Each of us kept a diary of Che's last revolutionary venture. The diaries of the other two finished up in the spotlight. Their notes, like *empanadas* crammed with chopped meat, eggs, olives, raisins and other tasty morsels, were consumed quickly. They added a good deal to the notoriety and charisma surrounding our leader's South American tactics. There was little room left for my account of Che's fate. But a time would come, I always felt, when my version of what had occurred would emerge from the shadows.

In that first moment on the terrace, Che clearly felt he had to speak as honestly as he could, even though his plans were still hazy. He was still working out where exactly the initial uprising would be. As we all now know, 30 years after the key events, he chose southern Bolivia. The blaze was set off close to the Chaco region, within striking distance of Paraguay and Argentina.

Some preliminary steps must have been taken before our comradely get-together on the terrace at San Andrés. It certainly wasn't very long before certain members of the group, code-named *Surubi* – the catfish – were sent to Bolivia as forward scouts. These included not only several new recruits such as myself, but also experienced guerrilla fighters such as Pombo.

The plan? Upon arrival in La Paz, we were to contact friendly parties, people who had been previously sounded out. Mario Monje was one, secretary of the Bolivian Communist Party. Tania Bider another, an Argentinian-born secret agent. She had been in La Paz for a while, getting to know influential people in the media and professions, infiltrating social groups. Leftish sympathisers could be useful in forming urban networks. My job? Spreading propaganda and subversive pamphlets. I was to draw upon the contacts Tania had made, carefully and very discreetly. It would be fatal if the Barrientos regime or even the CIA, which was rumoured to be at the President's elbow, became aware too soon how a revolutionary movement was taking shape.

So there it was. After crossing into Bolivia I found a room in the Sopcachi district of La Paz, a few streets away from Tania's place. I quizzed her closely as to what she had been able to achieve. '*Muy bien,*' she said, after a day or so of this. 'Let's press on – no if or buts.' She quickly introduced me to some of the editors she had charmed with her dark-eyed looks.

With Tania's help, I managed to publish several articles of the kind envisaged by our leader, moderate in tone, and supposedly of interest to the general public. My articles drew attention to governmental bungling in times past. Bribes and favours of that time, I hinted, were still being covered up, especially in the police force and the army. There were also rotten apples in the legal system. Notaries on the take.

With the assistance of a compliant broadcaster, I circulated some mildly subversive opinions on air, taking care at all times not to sound too extreme. Like satirists of old, from Juvenal to Cervantes, I portrayed myself as simply a decent fellow, a well-meaning Don Quixote, wishing no harm, but forced by conscience to try and remedy certain faults in contemporary society, minor flaws admittedly, but capable of causing irreversible harm if left to fester by officialdom.

All of this reflected the tactics outlined by Che on the terrace. In various ways I portrayed the Bolivian involvement in the Chaco war as a fiasco.

I reminded my readers that the war began when Standard Oil, with the backing of the United States and a compliant Bolivian government, sought to exploit the resources of the Chaco region in Paraguay. Officers in the upper ranks of the Bolivian army, led by General Hans Kundt, were outclassed, which led eventually to Paraguay regaining disputed territory. This debacle, I suggested, as Che had counselled me on the terrace, was almost certainly due to the Bolivian government's inability to resist the greedy habits of an imperial power. I let my readers know, by apparently casual asides, that this sort of thing was probably still going on, many years after the treaty that was supposed to have ended the war.

Outsiders and untrustworthy people at the top, I hinted, were subverting social values. They were a threat to local customs and culture. They couldn't be trusted to offer a libation to Pachamama or any other deity. They were blind to the ways of the Bolivian people. They were no good. Some were said to have close ties to German mercenaries, former Nazis perhaps. Others were said to be in the pocket of the American high command. I even went as far as to plant a rumour that when General Barrientos feared he had suffered a heart attack, soon after his election in 1964 as President of Bolivia, the CIA had immediately sent a highly-regarded cardiologist from Miami to examine him.

It was hard to measure the effect of these articles. I was gratified on one occasion, while attending a gathering of local artists organised by Tania and her friend Canela Dochera at the premises of their so-called Folk Art and Ceramics Society, to hear my rumour about the CIA cardiologist treated as well-established fact. It was passed back to me as the truth by the naïve young lawyer whom Tania and Canela had persuaded to act as secretary of their newly-formed folklore society, a body that was simply a front.

I had already worked with Canela Dochera. She too was from Paraguay. When she joined me in Buenos Aires after the Chaco war, we teamed up to run a left-wing broadsheet, an outlet for *avant-garde* works by writers and artists from Café Tortoni. I enjoyed being with her again in La Paz some years later. I saw the acceptance of my heart attack rumour as an omen, a sign that progress was being made in casting doubt on the legitimacy of the Bolivian government. And there were other signs. Student leaders were becoming inclined to mock the pretensions of their elders. They were taking an interest in our cause: the clearing out of colonial rot by the overthrow of oppressive rule.

The first steps had been taken in the formation of an urban network, a secret force that would be of assistance to Che in the fostering of discontent in rural areas, amongst *campesinos* and *indigenas originarios*. It gradually dawned upon me, however, as I pressed on, that my infiltration of the local media outlets had a down-side, an adverse consequence that Che might not have foreseen when he placed a pen in my hand instead of a gun.

He thought that I was well-equipped to undermine the government's authority by recalling the mistakes of the Chaco war. But as Tania and Canela eventually pointed out, this tactic wasn't actually so clever. It was a mistake on Che's part – and mine too.

Certainly, Bolivia's defeat in the Chaco war was a means by which the present regime could be defamed and possibly weakened. By noting poor judgments. By recalling corruption and incompetence at the highest levels. By pointing to pockets of decay that probably still existed. But this approach, I gradually discovered, set up a degree of resistance to the message I was trying to get across, not so much amongst progressive thinkers in the cafés and basement bars, from whom support could always be expected, but amongst business and professional people. It also annoyed certain editors and journalists, especially those on the right or in the political centre. They saw themselves as patriots. The Chaco war, with its Bolivian defeat, was over. It was behind them. They didn't want to hear any more about it.

They certainly didn't want to hear about it from the insensitive pen of a Paraguayan-born journalist like me. Why listen to Marvic Laredo? An outsider from Buenos Aires who was apparently taking special pleasure in reminding people of Bolivia's defeat.

Worse, I was then identified as a writer who had not only been a combatant on the Paraguayan side but also had gained a certain notoriety at that time as one of the so-called Paraguayan 'boy soldiers', heroic teenage combatants at the siege of Cosmequet. It was there, in the aftermath of a disastrous battle, when the Bolivians under General Kundt had to abandon their attempt to establish a port on the Paraguay River, that Bolivia was left as a land-locked country without access to any sea.

In a small city like La Paz, news of my background, circulated by one or two reporters who knew me slightly from Café Tortoni, had quickly spread. My attempt to convince people, even those who favoured what I had to say, that I had moved on was all to no avail. My previous history, the boy soldier known as *El Australiano*, was used against me.

I could argue that in the final phase of the Chaco war, even before the treaty to end it was signed, I had fled to Argentina, desperate to escape what had proved to be one of the most pointless conflicts of our time. I could attest that I had spent most of my adult life in Buenos Aires. No matter. All too quickly, I became known as simply a cynical hack from across the border, casting about for any old story to feed a column.

This was unfair, of course, for I had worked for *El Diario* and other respectable papers. I had credentials. But it was no use. To people in La Paz, even to my confidants and allies, as my old friend Canela Dochera had warned me, my Paraguayan birth and link to Australian settlers had become a liability.

I made no further mention of the Chaco war in my writings. I began using a *nom de plume* when a columnist's name was required.

Even so, it became increasingly clear that further steps had to be taken. I had to amend my characterisation as an outsider. It wasn't long before all of those in our clandestine network in La Paz had a clear understanding that my undercover role had to be concealed.

This was probably conveyed to them by Pombo, or perhaps by cables from Che himself, in Havana. My name, even the occasional *nom de guerre*, anything that might identify me, was never to be mentioned, not in conversation and certainly not in writing.

This rule was strictly observed. It's not surprising, then, that you will find no mention of Marvic Laredo in the letters or diaries written in those dangerous days. Nowhere, not even in the diaries of Pombo, Tania or Che himself. Not because they harboured any ill-will towards me – quite the contrary – but simply because they could see that my identity and any knowledge of my association with the inter-continental revolutionary cause could be a hindrance.

This was underlined when it became certain, with no possibility of turning back, that the revolution was to be sparked off by insurrections in the rural areas of southern Bolivia. *Guerra de guerrillas* down there would pave the way to a seizure of power in the main cities: La Paz, Sucre, Potosi, Cochabamba and Santa Cruz.

My cloak of anonymity was after a while taken for granted. *No mention is to be made of Marvic Blas Laredo.* That's the rule. Not even by use of an alias. You may see his name attached to a newspaper column. You may be introduced to him at a radio station or at the launching of a book. But all of that is simply a façade to satisfy the workaday world that he is what he says he is: a journalist from Buenos Aires. As to what goes on beneath the surface, as to his links to supporters of the cause, his fellow guerrillas, Laredo doesn't exist.

I must have been seeing too much of Canela Dochera, for she was soon protected in much the same way – at liberty to move about in public, in the workaday world, but never to be named or identified in secret despatches as to her assignments after dark.

Even Rolando, so indiscreet at times, was scrupulous in obeying Che's edict and made no mention of Canela or me. You will find no references to us in his diary. Unfortunately, his diary was brought to an abrupt end soon after the guerrilla campaign got under way. He was gunned down in an ambush at Meson by a bunch of Bolivian conscripts.

The hard but valuable lesson was there for me to absorb. *Prudencia.* If Rolando could keep my name hidden, be ready to swear on a stack of bibles that he didn't know, and had never known, Canela Dochera or Marvic Blas Laredo – the journalist from Buenos Aires, the former Paraguayan boy soldier, sometimes called *El Australiano* – then so could I. *No tengo amigos.* I was to be treated in our network as having no friends. Just a loner, a restless reporter who would soon be on his way.

It was for these very reasons, of course, out of loyalty to our cause, that I chose to keep my account of Che's heroic campaign entirely to myself. The fate that befell his courageous band of guerrillas was a tale for my diary, but not for others. The Paraguayan connection, my long-standing friendship with Canela Dochera: these were private matters. They were not for publication or for gossip. Only in that way could we be sure that the Bolivians we hoped to recruit, especially in the countryside, would not be offended by any possible reminder of the Chaco war or be prejudiced against us.

After it was all over, I put my papers away, doubting that I would ever look at them again. I kept them well-hidden.

It is only now, so many years later, when the time has finally come to honour Che Guevara by writing my article, I have brought my papers to light. I have been asked to join with others in a publication to acknowledge his legendary legacy. This means, of course, that I feel obliged to set out my recollections as clearly as I can.

Che Guevara was an inspiration to revolutionary idealists throughout the world, and many people would say he still is. He was destined to live the life he dreamed and his dreams are deeply embedded in the psyche of all those who recognise the necessity of effecting change by heroic insurrection. It is therefore desirable, as those behind the publication of my article have impressed upon me, that I give a satisfactory account of what I experienced while serving with him. I confirm that I have nothing to gain by doing so. I simply wish to underline the importance of everything he stood for.

2

THE MISSIONS OF CHIQUITOS

Ian Thornton felt obliged to sit and wait with the patience befitting an archaeologist of his experience. He assumed the unhurried air generally expected of anyone seeking advice from 'the Maestro', the portly professor beside him on the bench chosen for their talk. *Let him read the manuscript,* Ian thought. *Let him take it in slowly. The time taken didn't matter, not at this stage.*

To make sense of *Marvic Laredo's Article* on a first reading wouldn't be easy, Ian had to admit. The Maestro had been working on archaeological sites in Bolivia for many decades, and was well-acquainted with a host of influential people in all the professions and at every level of government. He would know many of the names and places mentioned in the article. But to take it all in, to grasp what lay behind Laredo's piece, one of the last men to see Che alive, was a matter that couldn't be rushed. Each step in this country had to be taken carefully, and the Maestro was bound to view his careful appraisal of Laredo's article as simply another step.

Ian knew that he would never forget his first journey to Bolivia. His undergraduate degree at the University of Sydney had led to doctoral studies at Harvard, followed eventually by introductions to post-graduates working on UNESCO projects in South America. It was then, while completing a research project at Cuzco in Peru, he was introduced to Kurt Meissner, an elderly German professor known affectionately to those around him as the Maestro. This had led to Ian joining the professor's archaeological team in Bolivia.

The Maestro was well-versed in Bolivian ways, the need for care in dealing with officialdom, securing sites and documenting discoveries. He knew how to keep rivals and dealers off his back by adding a bland veneer to site reports and a skilful gloss to his description of significant findings. He could read whatever was put in front of him quickly, but in case some polishing was necessary it was generally best to let him proceed at his own pace. Even so, despite this counsel to himself, Ian couldn't help keeping an eye on the number of pages remaining in the Maestro's hands, as one page after another was read and placed face downwards on the old wooden bench. The placement was done thoughtfully and with deliberation, as though all of Marvic Laredo's recollections were of equal importance, from the group photograph on the terrace at San Andrés to Che's downfall in southern Bolivia.

To wait patiently was necessary, but irksome. In addition to the crucial question – whether Laredo's account of what took place in Cuba and Bolivia so many years ago could be trusted – Ian Thornton was keen to hear his colleague's response to some related questions, such as the whereabouts of other writings concerning Che's final campaign, including diaries kept by Laredo himself. It would take the discerning eye of the Maestro, with his lengthy experience of the Bolivian scene, to unravel some of the ambiguities in the article. The Maestro had worked for UNESCO on various heritage sites, from excavations at the ancient city of Tiwanaku near La Paz to his current work on restoration of the Jesuit missions in the Chiquitos region. Matters bearing upon the fate of Che's final campaign were bound to be known to him.

The mystery of Bolivia, Ian ruminated, was conveyed not only by the incomparable beauty of its regions, from the shimmering heights of the Andes to the jungles of the Amazon basin, but also by the complexity of its past. This land-locked country at the very heart of South America was unique: a buffer state that kept Peru, Chile, Brazil and Argentina from having a common frontier. It was a troublesome neighbour to Paraguay on its southern border in the aftermath of the Chaco war.

There were other divisive features to be found in Bolivia. Each of its four distinct areas had its own character. The Altiplano near La Paz where Aymara peoples lived cheek by jowl with the *mestizo* middle and upper classes of Spanish descent. The Cochabamba district to the east of the high Andes dominated by the Quechua people. The region close to Sucre, generally regarded as the centre of the old Spanish culture. And finally, the wilds beyond Santa Cruz approaching the Chaco region, a remote area occupied by Guarani indigenes and a scattering of farmers from Paraguay.

The complexities to be found in Bolivia, ranging back to the arrival of the Spanish conquistadors and the Incan empire they displaced, and even further back to earlier civilisations, as in the ruins at Tiwanaku or the gnarled rock fortress at Samaipata. These had formed part of the Maestro's pitch to Ian while visiting the UNESCO site at Cuzco. *Think about it.* So many areas of Bolivia to explore. So many pre-historic sites to be investigated, several with potential to realign current academic orthodoxies, to shake things up. The elderly professor's dismissive gesture had seemed neatly to sum up Ian's growing doubts about the significance of the shallow excavation he had been working on at Cuzco. '*Davon geht die welt nicht unter,*' the Maestro had murmured. '*That won't bring the world down.*'

Within a few weeks of their conversation, Ian had been on his way to La Paz, keen to get going, to make a fresh start. A scramble aboard a crowded train at Cuzco set the scene for a trip of many hours across the barren and monotonous Andean high plains, to reach Puno on the shores of Lake Titicaca. A ferry to Copacabana on the Bolivian side of the lake brought him to a bus station and soon to a ride leading down into the saucer-shaped valley enclosing La Paz. The cluster of governmental buildings, office blocks and churches in the city centre was surrounded by a conglomeration of basic dwellings scattered across pinnacles of dun-coloured rock on all sides, a vast mosaic of fragmentary habitats rising to the valley's rim. The huge Illimani mountain loomed in the distance, capped with what was said to be everlasting snow.

The Maestro had been at the bus station in La Paz to meet him, accompanied by an Aymaran boy to carry the bags. They had set off on the short walk to the Camino Hotel in Plaza Murillo, although, from time to time, a hand to his chest, Ian's elderly companion had to pause to catch his breath. The Maestro had used these moments of respite to add a few footnotes to his review of the historic district they were passing through.

'Plaza Murillo is the main square. Old but usable.' His words and languid gesture suited the Spanish park with its timeless trees, ornamental shrubs and sculpted fountains. Some elderly men in cloth caps were seated on wooden benches by a band-stand at the centre. Gossiping, watching the birds hopping about. People strolling to and fro. As if they had nothing much to do.

The President's Palace and the Cathedral enclosed one side of the quiet plaza. Parliamentary buildings – the Senate and House of Representatives – stood nearby. The other sides of the square were taken up by shopfronts and little barrows attended by indigenous women wearing bright shawls and tilted bowler hats. Their stalls were draped with colourful fabrics or heaped high with pots and pans. A rough sign pointed to Mercado de Flores, the city flower market around the corner.

The statues in the sunlit square resembled apparitions from a canvas by Georgio de Chirico, sombre figures casting ominous shadows. The Maestro had stopped by one bronze figure, revealing, in the tone of a tour guide, that this statue depicted a former President of Bolivia, Gualberto Villaroel. According to a plaque attached to the monument, which the Maestro translated for Ian's benefit, it was here, in this corner of Plaza Murillo – a stone's throw from the Palacio de Gobierno and the imposing Palacio Legislativo – that a protest march turned into a wild insurrection. The Villaroel government was overthrown by a mob that seized control of the city. While the army remained in its barracks, they grabbed President Villaroel and several of his aides and strung them up on lamp-posts in front of the presidential palace. The Maestro pointed. On that spot, right there.

They had resumed their walk. Ian's guide went on to explain that the seeds of the insurrection leading to Villaroel's downfall could be traced back to the Chaco war, the four-year conflict with Paraguay that ruined the Bolivian economy, discredited the army, spread new ideas among miners and urban workers, and sowed discontent among the intelligentsia.

The process of social ferment hadn't ended with the overthrow of Villaroel. It had reached a high point in the 1950s, with upheavals orchestrated by activists from the mines in Potosi and Oruro. A widespread uprising led to a seizure of power by the Movimiento Nacionalista Revolucionario, or MNR. This had paved the way to radical improvements in the economic and political life of the country.

Needless to say, the Maestro observed, as they left the square and mounted the front steps of the Camino Hotel, the MNR was itself displaced in due course. The army was always somewhere in the background. Hence the rise of President Barrientos, the authoritarian ruler who had angered the left-wing regime in Cuba and prompted Che's ill-fated grab for power in 1967.

Ian's mentor paused at the entrance to the hotel foyer. There, with a faint chuckle underlying his German accent, as if to add a lighter touch to the history he had been unfolding, he pointed to a poster on the wall. Two horsemen. Butch Cassidy and the Sundance Kid perhaps. They were said to have stayed in this hotel soon after their arrival in Bolivia. The two outlaws, on the run from the armed robberies they had committed in America, eventually found jobs with the Concordia Tin Mines near Tres Cruces in the foothills of the Bolivian Andes, 75 miles south-east of La Paz. Further robberies had led to their deaths in a final shoot-out.

He rounded off the tale with another chuckle. 'A tall story, for all we know. But so what? *Pero que mi importa?* That's what the Bolivians say: *what's it matter to me?* It's a good story and it brings in the customers. The posters appeared when the Hollywood movie came out. That's history for you.'

'In this country, or everywhere?'

'In modern times. That's why I'm an archaeologist. Fewer fads and fashions in ancient days. The lone and level sands stretch far away.'

They crossed the foyer to the reception desk. While Ian signed the register and handed over his passport, the Maestro stood beside him, exchanging back-chat with the manager, mostly in Spanish. They seemed to know each other quite well. A few days later, Ian had found himself in a tiny plane, sitting across the aisle from his elderly colleague, as they flew to Santa Cruz. From there, with a broad-shouldered driver at the wheel, they began the long journey by road to join the Maestro's UNESCO team at the Jesuit Chiquitos Missions, an area renowned for its unique history and cultural riches.

They went first to San Jose where a German architect attached to the team was waiting for them, keen to acquaint the newcomer with the principal features of the place. Dominating one side of the main square was the mission complex founded in the 17th century, a defensive compound housing the Jesuit college. A cluster of schoolrooms lay behind the bell-tower and elegant Baroque stone walls of the church. They drove on to the Parish Church of San Javier, built in the same era, and finished up, a few hours later, in the quiet township of Concepción, where the Maestro was presently based.

All of this, to Ian, the newcomer, was enriching. The remote colonial churches, those at Concepción especially, constructed of wood and adobe, gloriously painted inside and out with swirling floral patterns, humanised by images of saints and angels, were a source of wonder. But not always, unfortunately. Within a century of their foundation, they had been cast aside, vacated in response to an official edict expelling Jesuits from the Spanish territories in Latin America. The churches had been left in a state of abandonment, still visible, not reduced to the lone and level sands the Maestro had envisaged, but condemned to a tragic process of disintegration. Fortunately, in recent years, the various churches and mission buildings had been gradually resurrected and restored.

It was an inspiring project, Ian reflected, seated quietly in the back row of the church at Concepción, still waiting for the Maestro to complete his appraisal of the Laredo document. It was now close to five years since Ian had left his consultancy at Cuzco to join the Maestro's team, but the time had passed quickly. Throughout those years he had worked constructively with the Maestro and his other colleagues, to facilitate the various restorations. The success of their rebuilding work meant that six of the UNESCO sites were now being used to host concerts forming part of the Festival of American Renaissance and Baroque Music centred in Santa Cruz.

Indeed, at this very moment, here in the mission church at Concepción, it was soothing to hear the music of a string quartet rehearsing at the far end of the magnificent structure. The wooden pews were surrounded on all sides by elaborate cedar carvings and ochre images. Behind the musicians flickering candles nestled close to the altar. Nearby, an archaic pulpit, decorated with gold leaf, stood upright, as if reviewing the quartet's performance.

It pleased Ian to recall that less than a year ago his half-sister, Anita, an artist based in Sydney, had yielded to his oft-repeated suggestions and made a trip to Bolivia to visit him. She had come to La Paz initially, going on to the Chiquitos missions. It had been a joy to show her the meticulous restorations of the old churches he had described in his letters. More importantly perhaps – for Anita loved music – she had been able to attend various concerts in the music festival. The Maestro and Ian's other colleagues had been helpful in showing her around and driving her to the concert sites. This had pleased him too. Anita could be argumentative at times (or 'contrary' as their mother used to call it) but each stage of her trip to this foreign country things had seemed to run smoothly.

When Ian drove her to Santa Cruz to catch the first of her flights back to Sydney, she had thanked him sincerely. Yes, Ian thought as they parted, everything had seemed to go well. But smoothly? Perhaps that was putting it too strongly. It was not so pleasant to recall, as he found himself doing now, that Anita's trip had prompted the complicated situation presently before him, the series of events that had led to him receiving from her a copy of Laredo's article, followed by a sudden flow of emails about the man who had written this intriguing account of Che's campaign.

Emails back and forth. Emails that had to be answered, each with a peloton of earlier emails clinging to the leader of the pack. *The recollections of Che's comrade! So strange! So enthralling!* Laredo's article, a piece written in Cuba apparently, many years ago, had become her latest passion. *I'm an artist! It's so fascinating! Tell me more!*

At times, as Ian lay awake, he wondered how to reply, not quite knowing what she expected of him. Casting about for guidance, he had asked the Maestro to read Laredo's document as an aid to solving his problem. But the more he thought about it, the more the problem kept changing shape. The nature of the issue to be resolved might well be the first question his friend put to him after he finished reading. It would be wise, Ian reflected, before the last sheet was added to the pile of pages between them on the bench, to make a further attempt to clarify his own thoughts. To work out a response to his sister's latest fixation.

It came down to this. Since making her trip to the Chiquitos Missions, Anita had felt she had to work into her art various South American themes. *Symbolic inspirations*, she called them, *iconic fugues*, art enriched by exotic musical structures. An artist friend in Sydney, according to the first of Anita's enthusiastic emails, had drawn her attention to the Australian settlement in Paraguay. Further research had led to an exciting discovery. Che Guevara's heroic guerrilla band had included an Australian from Paraguay. Marvic Laredo, born at Cosme. Descended from the Australian settlers. *El Australiano!*

A friendly curator, attached to a museum in Havana, had sent her a copy of some pages written by the man in question. Laredo's article! It confirmed their research. Enthused by all of this, Anita was now poised to enter a sculpted image of Che's comrade in a contemporary art competition being organised by the Art Gallery of New South Wales. To her, it was a perfect fit: Laredo's ties to the radical ideals of the Paraguayan settlement, and his link years later to Che Guevara's dreams. Connections of this kind were bound to be of interest to the competition judges. *Art and politics! In counterpoint!* This might well be enough to carry the day for her.

So Anita *had* to find out more about Laredo. That was the insistent message Ian kept receiving from his sister. *So fascinating. So weird. We have to fit the pieces together. Find a theme. Complete the composition.* Which was, of course, where her brother could be of use. He was not only an archaeologist, a student of history, but there in Bolivia, right there on the spot. She wanted him to leave Chiquitos and go to La Paz, or wherever else was necessary, to see if he could find Laredo. Or, if the man himself had passed on, find his friends. Track down, at least, whatever had happened to Laredo's diaries. Or any notes or photographs that might cast light upon his involvement in Che's final venture. The group photo mentioned in the article, for example. A print of that would be invaluable.

Delay could be fatal, she stressed. Laredo's article had been written in 1997 to mark the 30th anniversary of Che's death. Now, 20 years later, the 50th anniversary of Che's death was approaching. The more one knew about this weird link the better – and sooner rather than later. The museum in Havana had indicated that several historians and columnists were working on pieces to commemorate Che's life and times. *So get in first*, Anita urged.

Weird was a word, she often used, Ian reminded himself. It was also often used by the artist friend who had opened up the Paraguayan trail for her. *Weird.* The highest form of praise, apparently, in the contemporary art world. But where would it end, this quest for Laredo's legacy, the hunt for memorabilia of one kind or another? Was the prize worth the winning? To appease her, he had made a few enquiries on her behalf, but nothing seemed to satisfy her. The time had come to work out what weight, if any, should be given to this *el Australiano* riddle. The discovery she had made about Laredo's involvement in Che's downfall was certainly intriguing, but could it be taken further?

The Maestro straightened up. He put down the last sheet and, having done so, gathered up the pile of pages comprising Laredo's article and shuffled them into a neat rectangle. 'So there it is.' He stared thoughtfully at the cluster of musicians in the distance, as if trying to find some answer to the questions troubling him in the movement of their instruments. 'And your sister wishes to find out what she can about the author?'

'To help her in the Art Gallery competition I mentioned. And also, if possible, some further details.'

'Such as?'

Ian shrugged. 'Che Guevara's Bolivian campaign. Graphic details. About Che and Laredo and their fellow guerrilla fighters. Symbols. Images.' He let his hand float upwards. 'As in this church. Inspiration for a picture of some kind. A form or figure, or even a mosaic, that she could put to use.'

The Maestro's gaze had drifted back to the musicians. 'I have to say – and I will do my best to put this tactfully – that when I met your sister out here, close to a year ago, I was not entirely surprised to learn that she was an artist. A delightful person, of course, but restless. Talkative. I don't mean this in an unkind way, but a bit excitable at times. Impulsive perhaps. And not slow to voice her opinions.'

He glanced at Ian, then looked away. 'Do you think your sister knows what she's doing?'

Ian had to smile. It would be hard to argue with his companion's somewhat clinical summation. 'She's my half-sister, in fact. Nine years younger. We share the same mother. She's excitable at times, I have to admit. Driven by her enthusiasms is how I prefer to think of it. Her art. Her search for new ways of looking at the world. And she depends on me. Which is why I usually feel I have to help her. In case she's not quite in control of what's going on.'

'As in this case?'

'Perhaps.'

'We know a little about Laredo from his article.' To underline his point, the portly professor held up the sheaf of papers. 'But do we know enough about the curator in Havana she's been dealing with?'

'I know nothing about him. Or her, as the case may be. But I was hoping that your reading of Laredo's piece might cast some light on the information sent from Havana.'

Now it was the Maestro's turn to smile. 'I know the general outline of Che Guevara's final campaign, as most people do who have lived in Bolivia since the 1960s. But as to his comrades and the make-up of his guerrilla force, I know very little. I of course read Che's diary; I can recall reading Pombo's account of what occurred. Both diaries seem to square with what Laredo says. I've certainly read various articles about Tania's role in the campaign.' He grimaced, as if troubled by his next thought. 'Canela Dochera? Yes, I've read some of her fiery effusions. Like me, she must be elderly by now. But as for Marvic Laredo, I can't quite place him. Nothing comes to mind.'

'The name means nothing to you?'

He paused. 'Not to me, but that's probably because his links to the Paraguayan side in the Chaco war meant they had to keep him out of sight, as he mentions in his article. It was certainly true back then, and probably still true, that Bolivians don't like to be reminded of the Chaco war. And certainly not by a veteran such as Laredo who fought on the Paraguayan side.'

The musicians had lowered their violins, so Ian waited with them for a moment, before continuing. 'But you *have* heard of Canela Dochera. It seems to me from what you say that an approach to her of some kind might be the starting point. Which brings me to another matter.'

'Which is?'

Ian reached for his leather satchel. 'You will have noticed that Laredo's piece was published in a booklet. A collection of tributes to commemorate the 30th anniversary of Che's death. But you will probably have noticed also that it seems incomplete. Laredo finishes with Che's arrival in La Paz and a rousing appreciation of his leader's merits. He says little about the progress of Che's campaign in southern Bolivia.'

The Maestro nodded. 'A campaign that ended in failure. So Laredo may well have thought it wouldn't be politic to dwell upon that aspect of the matter in a celebratory publication. Especially when it was combined with the opening of a memorial in Cuba named in Che's honour.'

'There's some force in what you say. But could it be that Laredo's piece *did* present the full story? But that certain parts of what he wrote about Che's final days were not to the liking of an editor charged with the task of preparing it for publication?'

This was greeted with a wry smile. 'There has been a good deal of debate in recent years about the way heroic stories should be presented to the world.'

'There has indeed. Which brings me back to the editing.'

'I sense you are about to give me something else to read.'

'True.' Ian produced a second sheaf of papers. 'This appears to be a continuation of Laredo's article. But it was never published. It bears a pencilled note, *Marvic Laredo's Unpublished Draft*. It isn't clear who wrote that. And nor am I entirely clear as to where exactly my sister Anita obtained this document before sending it to me. For the time being, we'll have to assume that it came from the curator in Havana she's been dealing with.'

Ian closed his satchel. 'And we will have to keep this in mind also. If certain people, or some covert agency, didn't want Laredo's draft published back then, they may not want it brought to light now. I've warned Anita accordingly, and thus I feel obliged to say the same thing to you.'

The Maestro held out a hand for the pages. 'So be it. One never knows what havoc can be wrought by a few words.' He glanced at the majestic ceiling, the carved figures hovering above them. 'A few words from a Pope and everything the Jesuits had tried to do was swept away. Their well-intentioned attempt to reconstruct a continent? Consigned to ruin.'

'Until we appeared,' Ian reminded him. 'Inquisitive archaeologists.'

'Absolutely. Adventurers adrift in the uncertain past, the vagaries of the future before us.'

The Maestro rose to his feet and, as he often did with his field notes in the course of an excavation, tucked the extra pages under his arm. 'I'll study the shards and fragments in Laredo's draft and let you have my appraisal of the data. A few thoughts at least, as to what the mound of paper comprising this unusual site conceals or contains. According to Jorge Luis Borges, our inscrutable but widely-admired scholar from Café Tortoni in Buenos Aires, the solution of a mystery is often less memorable than the approach to it, our appreciation of the question confronting us, a first glimpse of the steps to be taken in avoiding pitfalls at the heart of the maze. On this occasion, however, I'm looking forward to reaching an answer to the riddle. What went wrong? Why wouldn't they publish Laredo's draft? Did he say too much or not enough?'

Ian's confidant paused to add a final thought. 'As I have often explained in urging you to add a few dashes of colour to your site reports, one has to persuade. Which is why I generally manage to emerge from the inner recesses of a site with a few connecting threads, or a plausible interpretation of the data, if nothing else. So leave me in the labyrinth for a while to make what I can of the recollections comprising Laredo's draft, the words and phrases he employs, and the echoes behind them. I'll study the data carefully and see if I can come up with some lines of enquiry that can be put to use.'

3

MARVIC LAREDO'S UNPUBLISHED DRAFT

Entonces. So there it is. I have said more than enough about Che's training camp in Cuba and all that. I move now to when Che turned up in La Paz, a balding businessman, still in disguise. He went straight to the *surubi,* the catfish, who had been sent ahead to create an urban network and spread dissent: Tania, Pombo, Canela Dochera. And me too, Marvic Laredo. Although, by this time, November 1966, I was keeping my name quiet.

Tania, born in Argentina of German descent, was passing herself off as Laura Guttierrez Bauer. A poor girl supposedly, teaching foreign languages, although to some of us she looked too voluptuous simply for that. But no matter, her looks suited the other part she had to play. *Una diplomática.*

In the year she had been in La Paz, she had done well. On the back of introductions from her students, she had met *indigenas originarios* from the Altiplano, then *politicos* in the heart of the city, smiles and a flash of dark eyes at the ready wherever she went. Her contacts included artists linked to the so-called Folklore and Ceramics Society, a front worthy of sideshow alley that she and Canela had set up. Posing as folklore researchers, they had obtained letters from the Ministry of Education, badges from the teachers' union. Enough to legalise their presence in Bolivia. Even better, papers approving travel to the interior.

Che, like the ageing businessman he was meant to be, cocked an ear to all of this. *Si me gusta.* He praised them for what they had done.

Then we took him to Elvira Santos, a dedicated Marxist. She was well-known in La Paz for her work with the Communist youth movement, Juventud Comunista. Che liked that too. And there was another thing. Elvira was close to the editor of *Informacio Periodistica.* The staff were keeping Elvira fully informed as to what was happening in the inner circles of the government. Which fitted in with other things, for Canela was in touch with the Director of the Information Service for the Bolivian presidency.

Pombo had been working with me to fix things up with newspapers and local broadcasters, where we found outlets for my occasional columns and talks. Pieces drawing attention to the flaws of the President and his ministers. I did what I could to persuade the contacts we had made that Bolivia was clearly the best place to light the fuse for a blaze all over Latin America, as progressive thinkers had often argued. Other places, like Venezuela. Argentina, Peru? *Si. Si.* These, too, were poised for revolution. But they could follow later, one step at a time. Right-thinking people like ourselves had to stay focused. Pick the best spot for the first fire.

I spent many hours polishing these pieces. Took care the tone was not too extreme, the case for change persuasive. But the line we were laying out, we had to tell Che, was hard to sell, and maybe not so promising. The head honchos in the local Communist Party doubted power could be seized by a general uprising, especially if led by a multi-national guerrilla force recruited in Cuba. *Reclutas* of that kind. Strangers to Bolivia, just a bunch of outsiders. The Party hacks were shit-scared the line of action worked out in Havana would be vetoed in Moscow.

Che, of course, with Pombo at his side, was a sweet-talker. He had spent only a few short days in La Paz, but had already managed to quell some of these doubts, for the moment at least. But I have to say, thinking back after all these years, that his looks in La Paz were against him. *A balding businessman.* Of course, he always spoke with concern, as if he meant it. But it wasn't the same as if it had come from some handsome freedom fighter. Black beret, firm jaw and so on. The image we know so well today wasn't in evidence. Could a mere ageing businessman like this get rid of tyrants and bourgeois claptrap? *Nada.* He didn't look convincing enough.

At times in those first few crucial days, when I sat with Che and his would-be supporters, cooped up in my rat-hole of a room by the Witches' Market, I couldn't help wondering where the whole initiative might finish up. When Che waved his arms about and scratched his scalp in the heat, I thought back to that first fine moment on the terrace. The sun behind him, arms aloft as he told us what the future could hold. But there was no applause on this occasion, here in my tiny room, close to a year later. The local people just sat there staring at the frayed carpet, weighing up the pros and cons. He couldn't rally those around him by stripping off his disguise. Not in a city swarming with agents and informers.

Once, I touched on this. After a meeting when the people around him had listened but said nothing, before sidling down the stairs. *No importa.* Che's easy gesture of dismissal showed that to him their silence didn't matter. 'They will be with us in the end.' He reminded me that he had to keep his disguise on or be caught. He raised a finger to his lips. *Prudencia.*

My consolation was that Che would soon be leaving La Paz. He would move to the farm we had managed to acquire at Nancahuazu, south of Santa Cruz. This would be used as a base camp for the training of our guerrilla force. A launching pad for rebellions in Bolivia. A staging post on the way to uprisings in Paraguay and Argentina. Away from La Paz, I thought, maybe things will become clearer. The actor's props would be thrown away, a new script written, the path to be taken laid out in detail.

The strength of Che's belief in the importance of widespread revolution was never in doubt. This I have checked. It appears on the first page of the diary he started, soon after leaving La Paz to head south. He speaks of a new stage, of heading for the farm, the base camp. Upon reaching Cochabamba, still disguised, he and his offsider, a friend called Pachungo, travelled by jeep for two days. Getting close to the farm they stopped and looked for the best route to the place, to avoid the suspicions of a neighbouring *campesino*. He might think the new owners were coming in to make cocaine.

Pombo's diary says much the same. He speaks of finding the agreed crossing point on the banks of the Rio Grande. There, at sunrise on the appointed day, he found Che's jeep already pulled up. They decided to cross separately, then look for a place to spend the night.

They stopped in a small ravine where Che, still disguised, introduced himself to Pombo's driver. A brawny fellow, the driver was startled, then amazed, by the revelation. At the camp fire, with a stick uplifted from the blaze, he swore allegiance to Che. *Prendes fuego a la vida! You set fire to life*, he declared. *Guerra de guerrillas! Muy bien.* Here in Bolivia was the best place for it. *Right now.* He shook hands all round. Whatever happened, he and his jeep would be in it to the end. *Hasta las últimas consecuencias.* He would be there until it was all over.

They went on to the farm the next day. There, in the week that followed, Che took control. He inspected the approaches and vantage points. He sketched the course of the Nancahuazu River, mapped the ravines, checked the overgrown areas nearby. Then he got rid of his disguise, with a huge sigh. His hair, he told his men with a wry smile, was slowly changing. The grey was going back to the blond, to which it had been bleached before dyeing. It would soon go back to its natural colour. And his beard was growing too. 'In a couple of months' time,' he quipped, 'I shall start looking like myself again.' He pulled a face to amuse them. 'You will have to put up with it. *Se hace facilmente,* as my parents would say. *It's easily done.* I will write to them and say so.'

I can't add much more. In these early days, I was not yet by Che's side. Nor was I there when the *reclutas* brought in from Cuba and other places found their way to the camp. I was still in La Paz, pressing ahead with our propaganda, writing my columns, but *incógnito*. I worked with Tania and Canela to strengthen their folklore groups. But events at the Nancahuazu base camp and skirmishes in the region nearby are fully covered in Che's notes, plus the diaries of Pombo and Rolando.

Training sessions at the camp went on throughout December. More *reclutas* arrived, including Braulio, Coco and El Chino from Peru. Defensive works were put up, supplies stockpiled, aerials and radio facilities installed. Friction between the Cubans and those from other countries, especially the Bolivians and Peruvians, sometimes disrupted the completion of certain tasks. Insects were a constant nuisance – the gnat, the mosquito, the tick and the *maragui*. The lack of sufficient netting led to squabbles and more time being wasted.

They completed a tunnel for hiding anything that could be incriminating, details of networks, not only in La Paz but in neighbouring centres too: Asunción, Santiago and Lima. Che's good humour was generally enough to keep things moving along. The regrowth of his beard and the gradual reappearance of his natural chestnut-coloured hair became a talking point. It is clear from Pombo's diary that Che and his *compañeros* celebrated Christmas Eve with much merry-making. They treated themselves to a meal of beef and roast pork. They got drunk. They danced. *Cantaban felizmente.* They sang happily. Che read a poem he had written, which was praised by the two Chileans: Urbano and Braulio.

But celebration was soon replaced by a darker mood. Some visitors from La Paz arrived. Tania had brought Mario Monje to the camp, the secretary of the Bolivian Communist Party. Face-to-face discussions became tense. Demands were made about tactics, the way things should be done. But Che wouldn't agree. He wouldn't give up his leadership of the guerrilla movement. It became clear that support from the Communists was now unlikely.

There was another complication. The signs were that it would be hard to recruit local *indigenas originarios* to the cause. Language was a difficulty. The group's training had included some lessons in Aymaran and Quechuan but it turned out that native communities in the Nancahuazu region were not of Aymaran or Quechuan descent. They were mostly of Guarani descent, and spoke Indian dialects unintelligible to the Cubans, and not known even to most of Che's Bolivian guerrillas.

Early in 1967, that fateful year, Che led his *reclutas* on a wide-ranging reconnaissance trek, another phase of their training. Unfortunately, at about that time, an advance party of the Bolivian army, responding to rumours about a foreign force close to the still-disputed Chaco region, chanced upon Che's temporarily-vacated base camp, and searched it. They captured two deserters and made them talk. What they said was enough to alert President Barrientos to the risk of attack in southern Bolivia. He called for assistance from the CIA.

It is greatly to Che's credit that, despite these problems, towards the end of March, he and his band of guerrillas fought back. They ambushed Bolivian troops in the vicinity of Nancahauzu in the first significant battle of the revolutionary campaign. This victory gave him some breathing space. Che set to work on a manifesto for what he now called the National Liberation Army of Bolivia, his plan to drag the United States into a never-ending war in South America, as now seemed to be happening in Vietnam.

Entonces. To finish the writing wasn't easy. Che and his men had to keep moving, scrounging food from sullen *campesinos*, constantly fearing betrayal. Their numbers were gradually reduced by losses in battle and further desertions. Army planes had begun to scan the guerrilla zone, bombing haphazardly, here and there, with no direct hits, but enough to keep the guerrillas scrambling for cover, always on the move, scarcely sleeping.

Then, while Che was still working on his manifesto, Tania brought some unexpected visitors to his latest hideout. An Argentinian artist, Ciro Bustos, and the radical French philosopher Regis Debray, friends of Canela Dochera. These two men were keen to support the cause, but they had to be fed. Worse, when Bustos and Debray sought to make their way out of the contested zone, they were captured by the army. It's now widely believed that papers on them – especially sketches made by Bustos – contained information valuable enough to satisfy the army and the CIA that the guerrilla insurgents were definitely led by the infamous Che Guevara. It was a Cuban venture which had to be crushed.

By this time, as we now know, losses due to betrayals, captured radio transmitters and various mishaps had left Che without any way of communicating with Fidel Castro in Havana. No assistance would come from there. This sapped morale. And there was another thing. A decision was made to split the guerrilla force into two groups: a primary band under Che and Pombo and a separate contingent led by Joaquin.

Tania, contrary to her leader's wishes, had stayed on at Che's hideout after Bustos and Debray had departed. She was fed up with sitting at Canela's desk apparently, planning and writing articles. She felt she had to fight. This led to a profound difference of opinion with Che. He tried to send her back to La Paz – but she wouldn't go. Their quarrel ended with Tania going off to serve with Joaquin's group. Che was downcast, deprived of her company and her advice. Now attached to the other group of insurgents, facing the challenges, she could only help those around her. To stay alive, she had to look after herself. They were both adrift.

In mid-July, Che's group made a desperate raid on the township of Samaipata. Medical supplies were needed for Che's chronic asthma. They managed to overpower the local garrison and fight their way through to the central plaza. They ransacked a few shops, found what they wanted, and dug in. But this didn't solve anything. By this time contact between the two guerrilla groups had ceased. I can vouch for this, for while Che was at Samaipata I drove in by jeep from Santa Cruz to join his force. I could see from the faces around me, and from what I was told, the force we had started with was now not only split in two, but very seriously weakened. The pair of Bolivian *reclutas* I had brought with me, the best I could manage in response to Che's urgent plea for reinforcements, was another reminder that our venture was in trouble.

We quit Samaipata. Che kept trying to contact Joaquin's group. But without a workable transmitter, communication proved impossible. To keep abreast of what was happening, we were down to scraps of information from the radio. In that way, terrible news reached us towards the end of August. Betrayals by *indigenas originarios*, mostly Guarani peasants, had led to the army mounting an ambush by the river crossing at Vado del Yesco.

Just before sunset, partly concealed by the gathering dark, Joaquin's group, with Tania towards the front of the line, started wading across the rapidly-flowing stretch of shallow water, with water up to their chests, rifles held high. At once they were mowed down by waiting marksmen. According to a news flash, bodies were swept downstream and only recovered days later. Tania's body was one of them.

We were numbed by what he had heard. Che was especially distraught. He had told Tania many times, his friend and trusted ally for so long, that she was not to risk her life in the wilds. She had been meant to leave his hideout with Bustos and Debray. She had been meant to join Canela and the others in La Paz. There she would have been of greater use to the cause than firing bullets in the wilds. But his plea had been in vain. She simply wouldn't listen. She had shoved a letter in his pocket, a note to her dear friend Canela, and left him. For Joaquin's group. And now she was lost to us all.

We were not to know it then, hunched over our radio beside the trail back to Nancahauzu, that what we had just heard signalled the end of Che's dream. Not just for those who had died in the bloody ambush at the river crossing. But generally. For the entire venture, his dream of a widespread Latin American uprising.

As the leader of the one remaining guerrilla group, Che, wracked by asthma, was reduced to riding on a mule. This was the only way to cope with his disabling condition. Disheartened by casualties and further desertions, he must have known the path was narrowing. We were encircled by an increasingly purposeful army. There seemed no way out. Our group had dwindled to what was little more than a band of vagabond marauders, cut off from our base camp, with no way of getting to our previously-concealed supplies. Just wandering through the rugged wilderness of southern Bolivia, fearing betrayals. The phrase for native cunning, *la malicia indigena*, kept coming to our lips, the word *sabotaje* to our parched throats, as we began to mutter about those who were meant to be helping us, back in La Paz, and elsewhere.

I knew from the comments Che let slip from time to time that he was well aware of our predicament. I happened to be with him one evening when he had just completed an entry in his diary for the end of September. He showed me what he had said. *The situation is the same as last month except that now the army appears to be more effective in its actions. The peasants do not give us any help and they are turning into informers.*

Why let me see what he had written? Was he seeking reassurance that his tactics were correct? Or had he recalled that in addition to bringing recruits to Samaipata, I had brought bad news? The CIA had set up a Green Beret counter-insurgency team on a sugar plantation near Santa Cruz. His diary note about the improved efficiency of the Bolivian army suggested the CIA's methods were working.

When I handed the diary back to him, Che muttered: 'Green berets!' Then he smiled and touched his forehead, as if to remind us both of better days, when his own beret was new. But there was nothing useful I could say by way of reply, so I simply nodded, and turned away. Che was remote at times, in conversing with his men, and even while we were camped in wild places. He spent many hours alone with his books and journals, but he kept his sense of humour to the very end.

We pushed on to the little village of Alto Seco. Here we were seen simply as a ragged band of outsiders, treated with what Che called in his diary 'a mixture of fear and curiosity'. We camped by the local waterhole. Bought some edibles from a woman's barrow. That afternoon, at the schoolhouse, Che and Pombo spoke to a cluster of peasants about the aims of the revolution. When the teacher's back was turned, a boy listening at the window whispered in my ear. The teacher couldn't be trusted. *He's a fox.* That night, on the radio at our encampment, we heard a press conference. President Barrientos and his aide, General Ovando, spoke gleefully about the cutting down of Joaquin's group at the river crossing. Papers on the bodies, they said, would be of use in trapping what was left of the foreign warmongers.

We turned to Che as we listened to this, but he simply shrugged and turned away. *No importa.* He gave no outward sign of dismay.

We left the encampment at dawn and went on to a ranch at Loma Larga. It was no good there, so we marched on to an even smaller one at Pujio. People fled when they saw us. We stayed longer at this second place. We were exhausted by the long marches that didn't seem to accomplish anything. Our days were disappearing into cliffs and ravines and empty valleys. But the sun kept coming back each day, dumping its heat on our heads. *Que calor.* Until it left us at night on yet another darkened track. Che, still resolute, needed rest, struggling to control his asthma.

On 7 October, as appears in the final entry of his diary, the eleventh month of the guerrilla campaign was completed. That day, we chanced upon an old woman grazing her goats. We seized her and questioned her. She kept a straight face and claimed to know nothing about the whereabouts of soldiers. When we took her back to her little shack, it turned out she had two daughters, one a dwarf, the other crippled. We gave her 50 pesos, telling her not to say a word to anyone. But the way she looked at us! A wizened brown face without expression. Flanked by the two stricken beings at her side, staring upwards, as if to pass on the ruin in their eyes.

So there we stood, and there she was, this sombre woman, thick-set and quite still, with a face like the old wooden door beside her. She held her hand out again, so we gave her a few more pesos. That done, we left. We doubted that she would keep her word. We turned away from the alien mood in that shack, without hope, not a word between us, feeling doomed.

We moved on at nightfall under a sliver of moon, Che seated unsteadily on his mule. There were no other houses in the canyon, but here and there we stumbled across patches of potato plants, watered by ditches. We lay down eventually as if time itself had petered out. It now seemed useless to proceed further. There was nowhere else to go.

We had reached the place where two small streams, the Churo and the San Antonio, met. We were some distance down the Churo ravine, four miles, maybe, from the township of La Higuera. It was here, at first light, that we were cornered by a bunch of Bolivian rangers, led by Captain Prado. It was here by the streams in that rocky place, on Prado's orders, a section of his force, using mortars, began shelling our encampment.

When the first shell came down, at Che's command, we scrambled for cover. Pombo and others floundered across the stream to a rocky outcrop. Che and a quick-thinking recruit called Willy began scrambling up the side of the ravine, with me behind them. Then Che was brought down by a burst of machine-gun fire. His rifle was knocked out of his hands. He was hit in the leg. Willy dragged him out of the line of fire. *Lo hizo con rapidez.* And even faster, with my help, to the cover of a ledge. We sheltered there for a few minutes while the firing on the slopes below ran on. But when we moved again, not quite knowing where the enemy fire was coming from, we were brought up short, confronted by a bunch of Prado's soldiers. That was it for us. We could hear the battle still going on along the slopes of the ravine. But we were out of it. We were done.

They took the three of us to a gun emplacement on the ridge. They tied our hands, and stuck the wounded Che on a makeshift stretcher. From there we were bundled off to a schoolhouse in the dilapidated town of La Higuera.

Che was scarcely conscious by the time we arrived. But right away they tried to question him. When I protested, *the inhumanity of it*, Captain Prado shouted at me. *No soy tu amigo sino tu enemigo!* Having told me plainly he was not my friend but my enemy, he called up two of his men. They shut Willy in a room at the end of the schoolhouse. They dragged me across to an adobe outhouse on the far side of the square. They probably didn't want any witnesses to what was said and done to Che, his fate.

I am well aware of the wide-ranging controversy of later years about what happened after Che was captured. What orders were given? And from where did they come? It seemed to me at the time, from the whispering around me, back-chat between our captors before they dragged me away, that Captain Prado was waiting for a message of some kind.

Everyone knew, including Che himself, that if they held him prisoner and brought him to trial, there would be never-ending uproar, all over the place. This was happening with the trial of Regis Debray, captured after leaving our camp in May. One way or another, or so it seemed from the whispering I overheard, the Bolivian high command had wanted to make it clear to the world that it was *they* who had beaten Che Guevara in battle. It was they, and they alone, who would now decide what to do: whether to let him die from his wounds or get rid of him quickly. To let the Green Berets, or the CIA, or any other American agency, claim the credit, would be fatal.

These were the problems worrying Captain Prado – but it didn't stop his men celebrating the capture of their famous enemy. Their shenanigans carried on most of the night. From the back room of my outhouse, *por una ventana,* little more than a slit, I could see them in the square. Swigging rum, shouting and cheering, caterwauling as they fired their pistols in the air, lurching around their bonfire like drunken devil-dancers gripped by the frenzy of *diablada* at carnival time.

Whatever orders Captain Prado got from higher up, and what actually happened at the La Higuera schoolhouse, is all still fiercely contested. I know this now. I can speak only of what I heard, and of what I saw myself, much of it just snatches and glimpses along the way.

When they brought me back to the schoolhouse in the morning, looking for answers, how many *reclutas* in Che's force and things like that, a baton in my ribs as they questioned me, I learnt that a helicopter had flown in from Vallegrande, with Colonel Zenteno aboard, head of the Bolivian Eighth Division. And also a Cuban called Roderiguez who had been brought in to identify their captive. Proof was needed that this was indeed Che Guevara, the famous rebel. Roderiguez was there also to photograph notebooks and other documents taken from the captive's rucksack. This was being done as they stood me in a corner to answer their questions.

Colonel Zenteno told me, first up, short and sharp, and without any sense of unease about what was going on around him, that Che had died of his wounds some hours earlier. *OK? You accept that?* With the baton in my ribs again, there seemed little to be gained by raising doubts about the body's identity, so I nodded. Said what they wanted to hear. The body on the table against the wall was Ernesto 'Che' Guevara. The notebooks on the table were his. Later, when I tried to say a few words about the way our leader had inspired so many people, the Colonel slapped my face. *Eso es todo por ahora.* That's all for now. I was dragged back to the outhouse.

An hour or so later they came for me again. The door of my makeshift cell was flung open by an angry guard. *No seas mala!* Told to behave, but nothing else, I was hustled across to Colonel Zenteno's helicopter. I waited by it with the guard while they lashed the body to the landing skids. Then, with Roderiguez beside me, and that terrible burden somewhere below, a short flight brought us to the Colonel's headquarters at Vallegrande.

We were bundled across to a building with a low roof and a sign saying it was the hospital of Our Lady of Malta. I sat with Roderiguez in the laundry area, while the body was being washed and cleaned. The Colonel and his men kept coming and going, questioning Roderiguez about what he had found in the rucksack. I was asked again if it was Che's body, but after that no one paid much attention to me. An hour or so later the body was laid out in the laundry. Roderiguez and others took more photos. These included a gathering of various officers around the table, with some shuffling between them as they jostled for a good position in the picture.

The laying out of the body in this spruced-up and scarcely recognizable form was done, I suppose, to make it clear that the man laid low by the Bolivian army was not a weak and emaciated outsider, just some maverick from the Chaco region, but a significant enemy, a real threat to law and order.

It struck me, even as the photos were being taken, that this cleaned-up presentation, these almost saintly images of the insurgent leader, could be looked at in different ways. The photos were supposed to document Che's downfall, a deluded revolutionary finally killed. But here he was, the rebel leader, now looking so good. A picture like that, it struck me, might well come back to haunt the group around the table, in a form more real than reality itself. Photos of this kind, like Korda's famous photo of Che Guevara in his beret, could be used to shape the minds of would-be freedom fighters everywhere, champions of the downtrodden.

The thought that struck me then was destined to become a reality of sorts. Images of Che have found their way on to magazine covers and coffee cups, even towels and T-shirts. An iconic call to arms wherever change, according to those who want it, can only be achieved by insurrections or upheavals. Che's purposeful gaze, his fighting spirit, is now buried deep in the soil and psyche of societies in every corner of the world, as symbolised by his re-burial in the mausoleum here at Santa Clara in Cuba on the 30th anniversary of his death. He will be long-remembered for a passionate belief in what he thought was right: the way in which an oppressive society can be changed from what it is to what it should be.

But most of that came later. On that fateful day, in the laundry at Our Lady of Malta, my thoughts about the photos being taken, and what might happen in due course, were not the main thing I had in mind. I was looking out for myself. And what I saw around me was mostly confusion, people coming and going in all directions, waiting to find out what would happen next. There was a lot of shouting about whether Che should be buried or cremated. Right here or somewhere else? Now or later? And there was other talk as to what exactly should be said about his death.

It is still a matter of amazement to me that, amidst the confusion at Vallegrande as to how Che's body should be dealt with, and as to what should be said, that I was able to escape. A miracle almost. Detained, ignored, shuffled to and fro in all the haste around me, I was pushed about from hand to hand. Then, quietly, with some whispering here and there, winks and nods, promises of bribes and favours by certain friends in the militia, I was suddenly at large.

It was a desperate time, admittedly. But it wasn't long before I found my way to Santa Cruz. And very soon, I was able to join Pombo and other survivors of the final battle, in hiding places arranged for us by what remained of our network in that city.

That first brief respite, the sanctuaries provided, couldn't last. Our friends and helpers soon opened the way to our only avenue of escape, a long trek over the Andes to reach an out-of-the-way crossing at the Chilean border. We moved on to a sanctuary in Santiago. It was there, unwisely perhaps, that Pombo, or Harry Villegas Tamayo – to use the name on his passport – made his widely reported declaration that 'the Communists did not support us, and that is why the guerrilla movement failed in Bolivia.'

Pombo's declaration was the first time this sharp critique was clearly presented to observers of Che's ill-fated campaign. It aroused the hostility of Marxists, and strategists in Moscow too, no doubt, but it pricked the conscience of others on the left.

In accordance with an agreement previously made with Bolivia's military regime, officialdom in Santiago felt obliged to withhold asylum from survivors of the campaign. Fortunately, certain locals on the left, sympathetic to our cause, took steps to ensure that Pombo and the rest of our little group could leave Chile safely. With the help of the leftist leader, Salvador Allende, arrangements were made to get us back to Cuba by a circuitous route.

We flew to Tahiti, accompanied by Allende. He introduced us to some friendly French officials. They had been following the trial of Regis Debray and were keen to assist. From there we flew to Sydney. Well-informed supporters in that distant city had been contacted in advance and made it clear that they would take us in. *Muy bien.* We thanked them well and truly, but in no time at all they started thanking us, some of them reviving slogans from their student days: *Hasta la victoria siempre!* Things like that. From our point of view, after all we had been through, the main thing was that they were welcoming and very friendly. They gave us one glass of beer after another.

When our Sydney friends heard of my links to the Australian settlement in Paraguay, and of my 'boy soldier' tag from the Chaco War, *el Australiano*, they pressed us to tell our story to the newspapers, but we declined. The fallout from Pombo's declaration in Santiago had made it clear to us that silence was the best policy for the time being.

They were disappointed – but never mind. Before we left, they treated us to a night of partying in a boatshed by Sydney Harbour. I remember it so well. A place on the foreshore. Moonlit waters and golden ferries in the distance. The massive bridge looming above us. It was unforgettable, such a gift to be talking to this one and that, and some of the local girls.

We were tempted to stay on for a bit, but time was against us, the need to report back. We flew on to Singapore, Colombo, Athens and finally Prague. A Soviet aircraft took us to Havana, where we were debriefed by senior figures in the security service. But otherwise, on their insistence, we kept what we knew to ourselves.

It then emerged that negotiations had been taking place with some American publishers, in La Paz, and later in Havana. It wasn't long before excerpts from Che's diary and other notebooks were being spread around. This led, inevitably, to various controversies as to what exactly had happened in his final days and to how his body had been dealt with. I could see that in these negotiations certain of my comrades from the networks I had helped establish in La Paz, such as Canela Dochera, and a number of her friends from Tania's Folklore and Ceramics Society, were probably involved and could be implicated. There might be consequences. So I decided to stay clear of it. I fended off the stickybeaks and gave nothing away.

I withdrew to Buenos Aires for a while, quietly renewing my former contacts at the Café Tortoni and other places. I looked up some old friends, those who could be trusted. Wrote some articles under another name. Eventually I found my way back to La Paz, and settled down, for that was the home of my closest friend.

Now, at last, on the occasion of Che's re-burial at Santa Clara in Cuba, in the special mausoleum where his remains belong, I have been persuaded to write this article about what I remember, drawing upon the entries in my journal to present my own account of those memorable days in southern Bolivia, so many years ago. In describing what happened I haven't looked for any financial advantage or sought favours of any kind. I am not beholden to any *facción* or political party.

I have read various accounts of what is said to have taken place at the end. Renditions of Che's final campaign vary greatly, as I am well aware. What is said seems mostly to suit the interests of whoever is calling up the past or seeking to interpret the so-called 'facts of the matter'. Some writers speak proudly of their role in 'truth-telling', laying out what they like to call 'the unvarnished truth'. For my own part, as I have said elsewhere, I have sought to keep my descriptions plain and simple, to focus on events I was actually involved in or saw quite clearly.

I judge my role as being a witness to history, in bringing to light at last my version of our dreams and misadventures. I am reminded by my diary entries that, almost accidentally, I was caught up in what proved to be momentous events. I am proud to have been included in a cause defined by one of the most outstanding figures of our time: Che Guevara. He was a leader oblivious to danger and discomfort. His only aim was to convert the South American masses to his revolutionary ideals.

His dreams were reflected in his actions. In the years since he died, his dreams have filtered downwards to enrich the soil of so many societies preparing themselves for much-needed change. He has left us but his spirit lives. His achievements will endure. I will round off my recollections with a passage from what was said by Fidel Castro at the reburial of Che Guevara's remains only a few days ago, right here at Santa Clara in Cuba, Che's adopted home.

A combatant may die, but not their ideas. What was a man from the US government doing up there when Che was wounded and taken prisoner? How could they believe that by killing Che he would cease to exist as a combatant? Now, he is not in La Higuera, instead he is everywhere, wherever there is a just cause to defend. Those who wanted to kill him, to make him disappear, were not able to understand that he would leave an indelible footprint in history and that his luminous prophet's gaze would transform him in to a symbol for all the earth's poor in their millions upon millions.

4

THE MAESTRO'S AGENT IN LA PAZ

'Senor Thornton.' The waiter from the hotel restaurant had arrived at last, the long-awaited cup of coffee on his little tray. He carefully placed the cup and saucer on the table and straightened up, answering Ian's smile with a faint smile of his own. As he walked away, Ian surveyed the foyer of the Hotel Mundus Novus and checked his watch. Still no sign of the Maestro's so-called 'agent in La Paz', although the local man was half an hour late already. But that, of course, was not entirely surprising, if Ian's usual experience of La Paz was anything to go by. Things often ran late, and seldom according to plan.

Ian reached for the cup and took a sip. Hot and black, but it needed sugar. He tore open the sachet on the saucer, glancing around the foyer as he sweetened the brew. Some tourists with bags on wheels at the reception desk. A woman in a floral blouse at the computer screen in the cubicle nearby. A sign opposite the revolving door at the entrance to the foyer had an arrow pointing to the lifts. That was all – save for a warning sign nearby from the Chief of Police in La Paz, a warning for visitors to the city. If they were obstructed in the street, or had liquid flung at them, they should be wary of accepting help from bystanders.

Strange advice, but necessary, as Ian well knew. Yesterday, on his first day back in La Paz, he had walked to the massive San Francisco Cathedral to deliver a note to the Maestro's agent, leaving it with an elderly woman at the front desk of the museum beside the church. Heading back to the hotel, he was pestered by a shoeshine boy with a battered satchel slung over his shoulder, full of rags and brushes. It took only a moment to say 'not now' and get rid of him. But even as he did so, Ian was immediately reminded of a similar encounter in this part of La Paz, a minor incident perhaps, but enough to show why a first meeting with the Maestro's agent had to be handled with care. *Hola! Hola! Hola!* Yes, the voice of the street boy had brought to mind not only concerns about the art project Anita was pursuing so avidly, but also some cautionary thoughts aroused by a previous incident in this area, plus the Police Chief's warning sign. *Liquid flung at visitors. Beware of helping hands.*

Ian had kept walking, straight ahead, doing his best to ignore the shouts of the street boy he had left behind. Even so, he couldn't help checking to see whether the boy had flung anything at him. A splash of maple syrup or chocolate on the back of one's jacket was only the first phase of a trick practised in the Witches' Market, a scheme to fleece tourists with the aid of a shoeshine boy.

Beware of helping hands. If passers-by in the street couldn't be trusted to render assistance, could the Maestro's agent and Canela Dochera be trusted to speak truthfully about Che's comrade from Paraguay, the reclusive Marvic Blas Laredo?

So much to think about. There had been no police warning sign in the foyer of the Hotel Mundus Novus a year ago when Ian had travelled to La Paz to meet Anita on her visit to Bolivia. The generally peaceful years he had spent working with the Maestro and his colleagues at the inland missions of Chiquitos must have dulled his capacity to handle the sharp practices of inner city life, the tricks for which he should have been ready while showing his talkative sister around La Paz. A blue sky overhead, friendly chats with the street traders: there had been no reason to suppose that anything out of the ordinary was about to happen.

When they stopped at one of the stalls lining a narrow street in the Witches' Market, quite close to the Cathedral, it seemed just the right moment to buy Anita a small gift – a bracelet from Potosi – and to dig into the back pockets of his jeans for some notes to cover the cost. But someone must have been watching them. The old woman on a stool at the corner perhaps, sitting there quietly with a red shawl across her shoulders, casually smoothing her voluminous skirts with an aged hand, keeping an eye on the line of barrows nearby, the trays of trinkets and racks of brightly-coloured cloths and shawls, watching customers and passers-by from beneath the slanted brim of her black bowler hat.

As they walked on, approaching the old woman on the corner, Anita kept chattering about the bracelet, as though she had never had a gift from her brother before. Should she keep it for herself or pass it on to her close friend at the arts collective in Sydney? But when they rounded the corner they were suddenly accosted by a shoeshine boy, his face concealed by a woollen balaclava, a wooden box for his brushes and tubes of polish strapped to his back.

Hola! Hola! Hola! He clapped his hands. Pointed to Ian's shoes, pointed to the box on his back. Flapped a grubby rag at them. All the time he kept moving to and fro, dancing about them, shouting noisily, and he kept it up, even when told *not now, no need*, he wasn't wanted. After this had been repeated several times, the boy muttered something and mooched off, drifting back to the line of barrows, as if affronted. This is what Ian took to be the boy's mood as they pushed on.

Then, a few yards further on, as they approached the next corner, a middle-aged couple, man and wife presumably, emerged from a doorway on the other side of the street and sauntered across the cobblestones towards them. They were dressed respectably, the man in a suit and tie, the woman wearing a pale blouse and grey skirt. Gazing at each other, they seemed to be chatting earnestly, unaware of what was going on around them. But then, upon reaching the sidewalk close to Ian and Anita, they became agitated. They pointed to the back of his jacket, where something was obviously amiss. With a few quick words in Spanish, the man urged them to stop.

'There's a mess!' Anita was somewhere behind Ian now, squinting at where they were pointing. 'Something brown and gooey on your back,' she exclaimed. 'Could be boot polish.'

The local woman dug into her handbag. With a delighted smile, as if to say 'here's the answer', she produced a packet of tissues. Without further ado, she and her husband began scrubbing the back of his jacket, with Anita struggling to assist. Abruptly, in the midst of the confusion, Ian found his sister at his elbow with a soiled tissue, showing him what she kept calling the gooey stuff, surmising that it must have been squirted on his jacket by the shoeshine boy, in a fit of pique.

The three of them kept jostling about behind him, ripping fresh tissues out of the packet, scrubbing away, until what they were doing seemed all a bit too much. So Ian told them to stop. The local couple seemed peeved by this. His attempt to thank them for their assistance and send them on their way was instantly eclipsed by Anita's flow of praises. She, too, seemed peeved by what he had said, as she often was when he judged a situation as getting out of hand, his lack of sensitivity.

She began shaking hands all round and gathering up the tissues the helpful couple had tossed in the gutter. Half an hour later, by which time he and Anita were back at the Hotel Mundus Novus, her mind still full of his begrudging display of thanks, Ian discovered that in the course of the scrubbing and sponging, the flurry of hands, the back pockets of his jeans had been emptied of the bank notes they had previously held, American dollars and Bolivianos.

When he made this discovery, he and Anita were standing in his room on the fifth floor of the hotel, waiting for the kettle on the bar fridge to boil. The amount lost wasn't large, small enough to allow for a faint laugh, a rueful joke at his own expense, for not telling the supposed 'helpers' to stop sooner, once he sensed that something about the situation wasn't quite right. 'The wrong people got thanked,' he told Anita, showing her his empty pockets. 'Our helpers and their accomplice, the shoeshine boy, should have been thanking *us*. A family outfit probably. Street-wise. All three of them.'

Anita stared at him, puzzled, shocked, indignant. 'What makes you say that? You can't just *accuse* someone. Your money may have got lost along the way.'

'It didn't get lost along the way. After buying your bracelet I put dollars in one back pocket and Bolivianos in the other. As I always do. They've disappeared. The only hands that touched my back were the hands of the two people who crossed the street to help me, and your hands. *You* didn't rob me. So the whole thing must have been a trick. The boy squirts chocolate. His pick-pocket parents turn up to create a commotion, and do the rest.'

Anita groped for a chair and sat down abruptly. 'They were trying to help. Trying to get rid of the mess.' She seemed almost tearful. 'They were just trying to assist you. Like I was. You can't blame it on me, or on yourself. So you fall back on accusing that nice fellow and his wife.'

'Yes, I suppose I am. And come to think of it, with you flapping about, the whole thing was probably made easier for them.'

She brought a hand to her throat, as if to check she could still swallow. 'Some poor people from the streets, and you accuse them – without proof. I certainly didn't see them take anything. They were just trying to help. You should be ashamed of yourself.'

The kettle was boiling now. Bubbling furiously. Loud enough to remind Ian that he had been in arguments of this kind many times before with Anita, arguments that couldn't be won and became increasingly pointless as resentments and differences from other days were thrown into the mix. It was time to lighten up, cool down. So he reached for the switch and brought the bubbling to an end. Nothing could be gained by deconstructing the incident, the case against the Good Samaritans, as they were to Anita's way of thinking.

'It doesn't really matter,' he assured her. 'Another lesson learnt. As it happens, they didn't get much.'

But it was too late for that. A wry smile and a few words to calm things down were never enough in these set-tos with Anita. She was taking off the bracelet, the gift to mark her arrival in La Paz, as if to free herself from handcuffs.

'You should be ashamed of yourself.' She dumped the bracelet on the table. 'I don't want it. It would be wrong to have it. From the mines at Potosi, and all the bad conditions there you told me about. Just money and pots of silver to you, but not to other people. You can't even buy something without accusing people of committing crimes, when the truth is that people like us are committing crimes against *them*. Tourists robbing the poor. Exploiting them. In the back streets, and all over the country probably. Trampling on their rights.'

Ian shrugged. He knew where diatribes of this kind would lead, bringing with them, more often than not, an appeal to standards reflecting what Anita always called their mother's wisdom, her integrity, her grit. These values, according to Anita, were mirrored in the autobiographical work their mother had embarked upon before she died, the unfinished typescript they had found in the wire basket on her desk, a story brimful of dilemmas encountered and lessons learnt.

But Ian wasn't in the mood for that sort of thing. Their afternoon had got off to a good start as they wandered through the streets surrounding Plaza Murillo and along El Prado, before reaching the back streets of the Witches' Market. He didn't want the day to end badly. It was he who had encouraged his sister to visit Bolivia, and now that Anita was here in La Paz, his job was to make whatever she was doing seem purposeful, and to keep her in good spirits.

While she ran on, defending the couple who had come to their aid, denouncing privileged people as social parasites devoid of empathy, Ian reached for the tea-bags and began quietly laying out the cups and saucers. He had heard it all before, although, on this occasion, there had been no mention of their mother so far, the one sure link between them. Anita went back to that quite often, as if to keep them on a trusted path, and possibly because it left little room for debate. Their late mother, she always said, was a fine and compassionate woman, and bound to see things as Anita did.

It was hard to argue with this. Their mother was indeed the one firm link between them. Otherwise, he and his half-sister seemed to have little in common. Anita was inclined to emphasize the link for that very reason, as a way around their differences.

The nine years between them made a difference. After their mother's death, before he had joined the Maestro's team and committed himself to the restoration of the Jesuit churches of southern Bolivia, he had taken it upon himself to watch out for Anita by casting an unobtrusive eye over her various pursuits and the ups and downs of her artistic life.

It was increasingly apparent from what she said and did that she was an excitable dreamer, elated one moment, in despair the next, constantly moving in and out of shared houses and ambiguous relationships. So many of her friends in the arts collective she had helped establish seemed naïve and unworldly, borrowing money from her and heaping praise on one another, although some of their art works finished up looking like the mess on their palettes.

There was no way of talking Anita out of anything. He was aware of that from past experience and various shouting matches. The best course, he had gradually realised, as a brother concerned for her welfare, was to stay in the background, to keep her feeling hopeful by listening to her outbursts and providing a helping hand when that could be done without fuss. The pieces fell into place from time to time, but the respite was usually brief, before she and her friends plunged into some new artistic fad or adventure.

He had been the lucky one in the family, he recognised, and that too had played a part in his feeling of responsibility for his sister. He had both a father and a mother as he was growing up by the Harbour in Sydney. A municipal librarian, taciturn by nature, his father kept to himself at home, attending to the books in his personal library, but he was a calm and familiar presence. Not surprisingly, he left the running of the household to his wife, for she, Lucy Thornton, was the lively one, always busy, involved in community groups, completing a degree that led to a teaching post at Sydney University, there at her desk in the front room, typing up her tracts and provocative articles.

Ian's father was not to know that in the years after his unexpected death in the early 1960s, his youthful widow would be caught up in the widespread unrest affecting university campuses. Lucy Thornton had certainly been left with a young son to care for, but this wasn't going to prevent her becoming more than a lively figure on the home front. A war-protester in the Vietnam era, an avowed feminist, her quickly-acquired activist credentials included a summer course on the Columbia campus in New York. While there, as she had claimed in her unfinished autobiography, she had managed to spend several months working for an underground press known as the Liberation News Service, or LNS. They worked out of a basement on Claremont Avenue, opposite Grant's Tomb, within a stone's throw of the Columbia campus. The scrappy manuscript she had left behind in the wire basket included a photo of herself, carrying her portable typewriter in its vinyl case, on the steps leading down to the LNS basement. A note on the back of the photo said: 'Little me on my way to the LNS newsroom.'

Radical ideology at that time, Lucy was fond of saying in later years, spawned many factions, brought about by sudden upheavals and often identified by their weird humour. Back in Sydney, as time ran on, the mother by now of a son and teenage daughter, Lucy's anecdotes about her wild days with the LNS in New York were eventually overshadowed by the cancer that took her life. Nonetheless, the mementos she handed down to Anita had included some tangible examples of the so-called LNS 'Manhattan humour'. There was a Dr Strangelove movie poster, altered to feature President Nixon in the title role. And also, a headline from the LNS paper she had worked for, blown up to twice its size, proclaiming boldly: *LNS Backs Rolling Stones in Ideological Rift with Beatles.*

For Ian, it was difficult to fathom what the boldly presented headline actually meant. This was possibly because his undergraduate days were too far behind him. If the headline was meant as a joke, it seemed a bit flat. If meant as news, or as an insightful observation, it seemed incredibly shallow. Not so for Anita. She was on her way to art school when her mother died. In the years that followed, wherever she was living, she had the headline on her bedroom wall. She wasn't in the business of teasing out meanings from it, she contended. The LNS comment on the Stones and Beatles could mean whatever you wanted it to mean. It was of its time, an up-raised finger to conformity.

Anita revered her mother. She often spoke admiringly of her formidable spirit and all her adventures. In the last years of her life, as her daughter was moving into adulthood, Lucy Thornton clearly appreciated these displays of admiration. But somewhere behind the appreciation, it seemed to Ian, lay a kind of silence, a fear of being discovered as somewhat smaller than the larger-than-life image she had conjured up for her impressionable daughter.

Whatever the reason, Lucy Thornton had continued to keep the identity of Anita's father to herself. It was never disclosed, save for an occasional intimation that, in the Vietnam era, their liberated mother had stumbled into all sorts of unexpected relationships. She was living in 'the moment' as she had liked to say, still finding her feet as an activist and finding herself. This was surely forgivable, and cast more than enough light on matters for which no excuse was needed. Back in the day, she had been on her way to a new horizon, to splendid dreams.

Their mother's stories seemed to be enough for Anita. She was outwardly unworried by the absence of a father in the household, and by the lack of information about him, although Ian never quite believed her. He knew where he came from. Anita was less settled, he always felt. He didn't find it entirely surprising that, when they argued, she returned so often to what their enterprising mother might have said or done about crucial issues if she had still been with them. The search was always for the kind of outcome she would have favoured.

When Ian was occasionally forced by dilemmas of this kind to dwell upon the vagaries of their mother's outlook, or when he glanced at the Dr Strangelove poster or the LNS headline in one of Anita's rooms, it was never clear to him what kind of credo he was supposed to be approving. He had been close to his mother in his school days, but they had drifted apart after he had left home. He was at his studies overseas when she died. Since then, and especially after reading her patchy autobiography, the only family issue he felt really sure about was that his sister would be lost without him. He had to stick by her.

Now that she was here in La Paz, he had to look after her. He brought their cups of tea to the table by the main window and sat down beside her, still listening to her defence of the shoeshine boy and his accomplices.

Way down below, he noticed, the plaza outside the San Francisco Cathedral was thronged with people. Smoke was drifting upwards from a scattering of small stoves dotted about the area. He waited until an opportunity arose to interrupt Anita's flow, then pointed out what was happening in the square. A performance of some sort. He could see a busker on stilts in fancy dress, surrounded by a crowd of local women in their colourful skirts and tilted bowler hats. Two figures in black-and-white zebra suits were dancing around the busker, saluting the man on stilts, waving their striped hooves at the crowd.

'The Zebra men.' Ian could see from Anita's expression that she was intrigued by this, so he carried on quickly, hoping to stem the flow of her denunciations by arousing her interest in something less contentious. 'They're part of a government campaign.'

'A campaign? What sort of campaign?'

'Street safety. Encouraging people to use care at zebra crossings.'

This amused her. 'Waving and gesticulating like that. They might cause some accidents of their own.'

'Possibly.'

'Zebra men! I like it.'

Anita's annoyance had subsided. In a way that was typical of her. It wasn't long before they were looking at their itinerary, the places to be visited on their way to Santa Cruz, and from there to the Chiquitos missions at San Javier and Concepción.

Since that afternoon, much had happened. In the year since Anita had made her trip to the missions, she had chanced upon Marvic Laredo's involvement in Che's final campaign. She had prevailed upon Ian to look for Laredo's friend, Canela Dochera. And here he was in La Paz. But the search could only be done with help from the Maestro's agent. Ian checked his watch and again looked around the hotel foyer. Still no one. He signalled to the waiter and sat patiently while the fellow removed his coffee cup and saucer.

What would the Maestro's 'agent' be like, if and when the man finally arrived? What could they dig out that would be of use to Anita in completing a work of art prompted by her trip to this corner of the world, inspired by Laredo's kinship to the old Australian community in Paraguay and by Che's attempt to create a new society? Was it really too far-fetched, encompassing the revolutionary dreams and disasters outlined in Laredo's writings?

Contemporary art was like that, Ian reminded himself. Much of it seemed far-fetched, with all sorts of wild concepts widely applauded. Weird shapes fascinated or shocked the art crowd. Eccentric ideas captivated the trend setters, from Tracey Emin's unmade bed to lipstick-smeared mock-ups of colonial sketches. One supposedly thought-provoking exhibition had featured tins of the artist's excrement. Serrano's crucifixion scene immersed in urine had been a hot topic in Melbourne not so long ago. If art was, as Andy Warhol had once boasted, whatever you could get away with, what might happen next? Was there a place for Marvic Laredo's image in this ever-changing mix?

He reflected that this wasn't the first time that Anita's search for a compelling image, inspired by some peculiar tale or fable, had led to requests (if not demands) for brotherly assistance. As an archaeologist, Ian was supposed to be an unfailing source of knowledge about arcane or unusual customs: Incan head-gear, slit-eyed masks. Was it really possible the trustees might award an art prize to a piece about Marvic Laredo, an award bringing with it a commission to install a sculpted image of the winning work above the entrance to the Gallery?

An outcome of this kind seemed unlikely. But Anita was hard to fend off, especially when annoyed by what she called Ian's 'negativity' – or, as she sometimes put it, by his pathetic bourgeois mind-set. But he knew he had to help her. He had to do whatever it took to keep her in good spirits. Nonetheless, he sometimes wondered, as he was now, whether at some stage he would snap, and simply say: *enough is enough*. Taking it upon himself to denounce the folly inherent in her increasingly bizarre view of reality.

While talking to the Maestro at Concepción, Ian had tried to explain his feeling of responsibility for his sister, and how this underlay the quixotic nature of his current quest, the attempt to find out more about Laredo. His friend and mentor had sympathised but having completed his reading of *Marvic Laredo's Unpublished Draft*, it soon emerged that he was keen to find out more. 'There's definitely something odd about it,' he insisted. 'Recruits like Laredo were mentioned in the diaries kept by his fellow combatants, including those of Tania, Pombo and even Che himself, but a man called Laredo wasn't specifically identified by any of them. And yet, in both the published and unpublished documents Laredo confidently asserted that he was a member of Che's guerrilla force. Fought beside him in the wilds to the very end. Managed to escape, and got back to Cuba eventually with Pombo and the others. What are we to make of it? Laredo's scarcely visible presence in the diaries kept by others is odd. A space in the jigsaw puzzle without a piece to fit.'

There was not only impatience but a strange intensity in the Maestro's tone. 'Your sister's quest is very odd. And the little we know of Marvic Laredo is odd too. There is no other way. You must go to La Paz. Forthwith. You cannot leave this mystery hanging in the air. And you will never forgive yourself if you fail to assist her.'

His plump hands went suddenly to his chest as if to curb a surge of excitement. 'I will give you a note,' he declared. 'A note to the man I call my agent in La Paz. A man who knows the back streets. He will help you locate Canela Dochera, and she perhaps will lead you to Laredo. Or at least tell you more about him.'

He lowered his hands and let them rest in his lap. 'So many questions unanswered! The ins and outs of Laredo's draft! Doubts about what happened at Vallegrande. Doubts about the proof of death and what was done with the body. Che is everywhere, Castro claimed, a legendary figure whose image has multiplied throughout the earth. But if Che has now become a kind of phantom, we must find out whether some of those around him when he died have re-appeared as phantoms too. Yes, I will give you a note. And a list of facts and matters to be investigated.'

The elderly scholar, calmer now, began to sum up in a level tone. 'When it comes to revealing historical truth, by research or by digging for it, so much depends upon interpretation of the data. For some of our colleagues, the past can be shaped by what they think today, and how they think it should be shaped to improve tomorrow. For them, spectres of the present haunt the past's imperfect empire, and have to be appeased. But for others, those of us who simply wish to work out what life was like in the past, and what people actually thought in their own time, facts come first. One must stick to the evidence. As in this case. If we are to get to the bottom of this Laredo affair, we must do so in an orderly way. We must measure the ground, mark the site, assemble the data, discard the waste, and present the case for whatever seems to be authentic.'

That was it. The Maestro's advice. Ian smiled wryly as he recalled the journey he had made in recent days in response to his friend and mentor's plan of action, the trip on pot-holed roads from the Chiquitos missions to Santa Cruz, and from there to where he was seated now, in the foyer of the Hotel Mundus Novus. The Maestro's introductory note had been delivered. Now his agent in La Paz was required to make his appearance.

What the fellow looked like, or even his age, was unclear. He would probably be carrying the yellow envelope containing the Maestro's note, the envelope Ian had left at the museum yesterday afternoon. What else did he know about him?

A man who knows the back streets of La Paz.

That was all Ian had to go on. A yellow envelope and a vague description. He rose to his feet and left the coffee table. The man could possibly be waiting in the noisy street outside, not wanting to be observed by hotel staff. There could be repercussions for being seen with the wrong sort of people. Especially gringos.

In a city like La Paz, it was known that anything could happen.

5

CARLOS QUIRIGO

The revolving front door of the Hotel Mundus Novus eased Ian outwards into the street, quietly but quickly, as if a broom had been used to brush debris out of the foyer with a single cleansing stroke. He wasn't sure which way to look, or even what exactly he was looking for. A vehicle perhaps? Maybe a driver in dark glasses and a baseball cap? Ian pushed through the crush of pedestrians and street vendors to reach the protection offered by a street sign on the kerb.

Opposite the sign stood the entrance to the Hotel Bolivar, a five-storeyed presence on the far side of the street, a backdrop to the flow of traffic edging along Calle Potosi in fits and starts. Cars, vans, taxis, motor scooters. The haphazard flow was being jerked forward, it seemed, by a cacophony of constantly-sounded car horns.

They were not the only contributors to the pandemonium. There were young men with faces masked by balaclavas, eyes within woollen slits, leaning out of the side windows of mini-buses, gesticulating and shouting loudly at people on the pavement.

On his first trip to La Paz, now some years ago, Ian had been shaken up, scared, by what seemed to be a bucketful of abuse being hurled at him by these noisy faces, ranting and raving as their vehicle careered along the street. Were they after him as a foreigner, a gringo? But the Maestro, his guide on that occasion, had quickly quelled his fears, explaining that these young fellows were paid by transport touts to shout out the names of places on their bus routes. Like shoeshine boys, they wore the balaclavas to avoid recognition, for many of them were students, would-be lawyers and doctors, or prospective clerks, whose careers could be tainted if they were known to have scraped together some pocket-money by working in such a way.

With this in mind, Ian left the kerb to scan the array of shoeshine stands flanking the entrance to the Mundus Novus. Benches and stools were laid out first thing in the morning by those who had paid for a position at this site, their places secured by satchels laden with brushes, boot polish and clumps of grubby towels and rags. He wondered whether anyone among the shoeshine boys had a message for him. While waiting for custom, they often ran errands or delivered messages to places nearby, or in the back streets.

To Ian's surprise, as he checked the shoeshine area, a middle-aged man in a leather jacket, who had been sitting on a bench close to the revolving door, caught his eye and smiled. He had a large moustache and bushy eyebrows. The fellow rose to his feet, holding up a yellow envelope. He flapped it up and down like a sailor with a semaphore flag as if to say: 'Is this what you're looking for?'

Ian nodded, for this was the envelope he had left at the Museum. He did his best to smile back as he approached the man. It wasn't pleasant to have what was supposed to be a confidential communication waved about in this way. He was still affected by the feeling of apprehension that had gripped since embarking upon his journey to La Paz. If Marvic Laredo had felt obliged to conceal his identity all these years, and had kept his unpublished diaries to himself, then he must have feared harm or retribution from those with a continuing interest in the truth about Che's final days. Here, outside the Mundus Novus, there were too many people around. A better place to confer had to be found – and fast.

'You have Senor Meissner's letter?' Ian touched the yellow envelope. 'You are his agent in La Paz?'

'I am indeed.' The burly fellow gripped Ian's hand and winked. 'I am here for the Maestro, as we who know him well in this city have always called him. I am Carlos Quirigo.'

'You can do as the Maestro asks?' Ian touched the envelope again. 'Confidentially?'

'Of course.' The envelope went into an inner pocket of the speaker's jacket. 'That's the way I always work.'

'I was looking for you in the foyer of the hotel.'

Carlos smoothed his moustache with a chunky finger. 'There is a small problem in that respect.'

'A problem?'

'Nothing so much to worry about. But I thought I should wait outside.' He smiled, as if at a private joke. 'In La Paz it is sometimes safer to sit with the shoeshine boys than with the politicians in the foyer. If you know what I mean.'

'I'm not sure I do.' None of this was reassuring. Ian was finding it difficult to keep smiling.

But Carlos seemed to be enjoying himself. 'The boys are only after your money. And they let you walk away afterwards. Poorer perhaps, but with your limbs and reputation still intact.' He placed a hand on Ian's shoulder. 'I'm joking, of course.'

Disturbed by wild shouts from a passing mini-bus, Carlos brought the badinage to an end. 'Let's walk.' He seized Ian's arm. 'I have set up a meeting with a certain lady. You're ready for that, I imagine?'

They joined the flow of pedestrians. They were on their way to Plaza Murillo, it seemed, where the government buildings were. Still disconcerted by his companion's opening remarks, Ian pressed him. 'A problem with the hotel? What kind of problem?'

Carlos chuckled. 'A very small thing. Inconsequential perhaps, but important to me. A fight about posters.'

'Posters?'

'You know the movie about Butch Cassidy and the Sundance Kid?'

'I saw it. A long time ago.'

'One of the few films in which Bolivia is featured. That final shoot-out in the courtyard. I saw it as a teenager and I've been hooked on it ever since. Paul Newman as Butch. Robert Redford as the Kid. I've followed their careers. And I know all about the facts of the matter. Actual and made-up. An incredible story.'

This was still puzzling. But it didn't seem to matter. Carlos had more to say. 'I told all I know to my friend at the Camino Hotel. Up there in Plaza Murillo. Including the likelihood that the two gringo bandits stayed at his hotel. Room 217. On the second floor. Way back in 1906. Before they went looking for work. Put a poster on your wall, I told him. A talking point for the tourists. Your customers.' Carlos turned to Ian. 'You stayed at the Camino Hotel, I believe. When you first arrived. Or so our friend the Maestro told me.'

'I did,' Ian confirmed. 'I seem to recall a poster by the front desk. Two men on horseback.'

Carlos spread the palm of his hand in what seemed to be a triumphant gesture. 'One of *my* posters. Butch Cassidy and the Sundance Kid. I found a place for them. Just figures in my friend's mind at first, but once he got used to them, a fixture on his wall. I printed a batch. It wasn't long before some other places went along with the idea. Small hotels, boarding houses, backpacker hostels, and so on.' He rubbed his fingers together to make the money sign. 'I kept everyone happy.'

'Except the Hotel Mundus Novus, I suspect.'

'True enough. I had a poster there for a while, but a new man came in and tore it down. Told me to stay away. Said he had done his own research. These two Americans were armed robbers. Best dead.

I've got customers coming back to me, he complained, with chocolate squirted on their clothes. Empty pockets. What will they think if they see a poster glorifying two bandits? I took it down. Two of the biggest names in Hollywood, I told him. Newman. Redford. It meant nothing to him. Just two fakes, he said, like the Butch Cassidy story in real life. Which led to another quarrel.'

Carlos placed a hand over his heart. 'I was deeply hurt. I swore I would never enter his hotel again. And I never have.'

'What did he mean? About the story in real life?'

'There was some truth in what he said.' Carlos chuckled at the thought. 'Although I made no such admission while we were quarrelling. All the books and articles seem to agree that the outlaw known as Butch Cassidy was a man called Robert Leroy Parker, born in Utah. After various armed robberies in the surrounding states, he fled to La Paz with his partner in crime, Harry Longabaugh. They left the Camino Hotel for jobs at the Concordia Tin Mines. But no one seems to agree on what happened after that. According to one report, two men robbed the pack train of a neighbouring mine, near the town of Tupiza. The bandits made off with bags of payroll money strapped to the back of a company mule, branded with the letter A. Soon afterwards, two North American gringos rode into San Vincente, a small Indian village. They paid for a room at the local police station which was also used as an inn. When a local vigilante noticed a mule branded A in the main street, he sent a runner to a nearby encampment of Bolivian troops.'

The storyteller paused to collects his thoughts. 'The shoot-out that supposedly followed, as shown in the movie, is a matter of debate. The earliest mention of it is to be found in the April 1930 issue of *Elks* magazine. A piece written by one of the magazine's usual hacks, crammed with blood and bullets. But in my opinion, and in the opinion of many others, no one knows exactly what happened at San Vincente, nor the identity of the two strangers. Some say they were buried on the outskirts of the town. Others say they got away. There were various robberies after the siege at San Vincente which local newspapers attributed to Butch and Sundance. But by that time, of course, their names were being used by bandits all over the place. Their notoriety may have led to their names being attached to the strangers who checked into the police station before the shoot-out. If the two strangers were in fact killed in the fight it would certainly have suited the troops and the local gendarme to claim they were indeed Butch Cassidy and the Kid. True or false, it would have been a feather in their caps. On the other hand, Butch's sister, Lula Parker Berenson, claimed that her brother returned to the United States, alive and well.

'Have any of these doubts and uncertainties quelled your enthusiasm for the movie?'

'On the contrary. I love the movie even more. The mysteries make it even better.' He made the money sign again. 'It isn't just the posters. The story contains enough truth to open up all sorts of opportunities. I've taken tourists and backpackers to San Vincente. There's so much to talk about. As it was back then. Bandits didn't have to pull out their guns. They could scare people into handing over their money by simply claiming to be Butch and Sundance. Imposters are what they have always been in this country: a cheaper slice of reality. Which is what most people want.'

They had stopped at a street corner. As they waited for a break in the traffic, an expectant look in the storyteller's eye suggested it was Ian's turn to explore the mystery, with a query as to the identity of the bandits, or a challenge to the story's authenticity.

'Why would two strangers to a town stay at a police station?' he asked. 'If indeed they were on the run? Especially if they had money-bags with them and a stolen mule?'

'Point well made. I have asked the same question – of myself, and of others. Many times. There are even doubts about the mule with the

A brand. Was there ever such a mule in the main street? Or was that poor creature invented later to excuse the deaths that followed? So many loose ends, eh? So many possibilities. My clients love to talk about things like that. Standing in the main street of San Vincente. Looking in all directions. This way and that.'

The years Ian had spent with his fellow archaeologists pondering artefacts and surveying half-completed excavations came quickly to mind. Where to next? That was always the question posed by a riddle. He had heard the blend of uncertainty and excitement underlying queries of that kind many times before. But now he had to steer the conversation in some other direction before it started going round in circles or disappeared into a vortex of supposedly crucial details that might or might not lead to answers.

They had arrived at the corner of Calle Potosi and Calle Ayacucho. The street sign, beneath a tangle of power lines overhead, displayed an arrow slanting upwards to Plaza Murillo. 'And your friend from the Camino Hotel?' Ian pointed. 'Up there in Plaza Murillo, I seem to recall. What does he think about all of this? Does he still have your poster on his wall?'

'He does, but in different premises now. You may well recall the overthrow of President Sanchez de Lozada some years ago. The *campesinos* feared he would sell Bolivia's resources of natural gas to foreign powers and cut the income of indigenous coca growers by enforcing Washington's drug eradication policies. When Aymarans from El Alto swarmed into the Plaza there were violent clashes with armed protesters near the Palacio Legislativo. Walls pock-marked by bullet holes on all sides. That was the end of the Camino Hotel. But my friend is now doing well in a smaller place.' Carlos gestured. 'A lodge on the other side of the Prado. By Plaza Aboroa. With several posters on his walls!'

A huge delivery truck had brought traffic to a standstill, so Carlos led the way across the intersection, still talking. 'You know Mesa replaced Sanchez de Lozada as President, then, as the new constitution gave more people the vote, came Evo Morales, the leader of the *indigenas originarios*. Of course, his followers now want more.'

As if to underline his point, Carlos drew Ian's attention to an array of helmeted police guarding the approach to Plaza Murillo. Their dark blue uniforms were weighted with firearms and truncheons, badges and buckles. Carlos lowered his voice. 'Yes, you still get your daily dose of demonstrators heading for the parliament. Brandishing their placards with the same old slogans: *El Poder del Pueblo*. As if power came to the people with the banging of their drums. But it can happen before you know it. By the look of that lot up there, shoulder to shoulder, walkie-talkies at the ready, facing placards and protesters on the corner, anything could happen. In the next few minutes.' He smiled. 'But fortunately, my friend, we are heading in another direction.'

Carlos grabbed Ian's sleeve and drew him towards a narrow, cobblestone street sloping downwards to the Avenue 16 de Julio. This busy thoroughfare ran right through the centre of the old city. It followed the line of what had once been a sizable river at the heart of the valley, a river now reduced to a watercourse in a concrete channel, flanked by commercial buildings and high-rise apartments.

'I am taking you to the Blue Note Wine Bar,' Carlos murmured 'Close by the Witches' Market. The lady you are looking for has agreed to meet us there. She is well-known in that area. And very influential. People know it isn't wise to cross her. Or to leave her with a grudge.'

'And what's your link to the lady?'

'Why did the Maestro turn to me? Not just because I have done odd jobs for him over the years – although that is part of it. Canela Dochera used my father as a driver when she first came to La Paz all those years ago. She needed a local man to find her way around. He had two taxis then, back in the 1960s. He called them his 'fleet'. Which in later years I always thought was laughable, with all their dents and scratches. But in those early days, to me as a kid in short pants, they looked just fine. Two battered cars that served him well. Enough to get the lady from place to place any time she wanted.'

Ian's guide came to a sudden halt beside a street barrow heavily laden with half-opened hessian bags, displaying nuts and dried figs. These were being sold by an Aymaran woman seated on a wooden stool. Without a word being said, her dark eyes calm beneath the brim of her bowler hat, she began spooning shelled peanuts into a brown paper bag.

'Gracias.' Carlos dropped some coins in her tin cup and, as he did so, with the ease of a magician, he slipped a cell-phone to her and received another in exchange. Both phones disappeared immediately.

This lightning transaction was effected without any change of expression on either side. What lay behind it, Ian wondered? An exchange of data on the phones perhaps? Or photos?

Carlos held out the bag of nuts to Ian like a magician offering a treat to a youngster in the front stalls, the mystery of his show, the secret of his dark arts, kept to himself. 'A little something to keep us going.' He poured some nuts into Ian's hand before walking on ahead.

'That's how it was,' Ian's guide continued, as though their conversation hadn't been interrupted and the bag of nuts was all he had acquired. 'I was too young to know Canela properly in those days, although I ran messages for her from time to time. Mostly an errand boy back then. But not always.' The thought seemed to amuse him. 'I was with her on the day of the special picnic.'

'A picnic?'

'We took both cars to the ruins at Tiwanaku, my father driving one car, my elder brother at the wheel of the other. Canela had some Germans with her. Archaeologists, I suppose. We had lunch quite close to the old Sun Gate, and it was all very friendly. A kind of picnic, which is probably why my older brother and I were allowed to come. An outing on a Sunday. But it seemed special because the visitors were mostly speaking German, which was a mystery to me. But there they were in their excitement, walking around the ruins in their big canvas sun hats, jabbering away, pointing their cameras at Lake Titicaca and the mountains in the distance.'

'Canela made use of my father's little fleet for things like that,' Carlos added. 'She became quite close to him. And when my brother and I were older, we drove for her now and again. But all this stopped when my father got sick and died. We had to sell the cars and look for work in other places. But she still calls on me occasionally. For odd jobs. Helping out as I do now for the Maestro.'

'And Marvic Laredo? What can you tell me about him?'

Carlos slowed a little, as if feeling obliged to speak carefully. 'Marvic Laredo. Now there's another peculiar thing.'

He popped a few more nuts into his mouth and chewed for a bit, keeping an eye on the traffic ahead. 'A very peculiar thing. Because I always have to ask myself: am I describing what I saw or what I've come to believe? Like so many others, I read the article Laredo wrote to commemorate the reburial of Che's remains in Cuba. Before I read it, I used to claim that I had met Che back in the 1960s when he came to La Paz. Like I said, my brother and I were running errands for Canela at that time, to and fro in the Witches' Market. Her friends certainly included a man who looked like Che Guevara. He may even have been one of those on the Tiwanaku picnic I mentioned. Needless to say, when Che's photo was in all the papers after the final battle near Vallegrande, we used to boast that we had run errands for the Cuban hero and his friends. And we made the same boast about Marvic Laredo when his article appeared many years later. Until the Maestro put some questions to me in that way he has.'

'What sort of questions?'

'Questions prompting me to take a closer look at Laredo's article. It's clear from what he said that while in La Paz, Che was disguised as a middle-aged Uruguayan businessman. That meant, when we came to think closely about it, that we could only have been running errands from Canela to Che's comrade in the final campaign. Marvic Laredo, the author of the article.'

The storyteller chuckled. 'But that was no good either. Canela overheard me making such a boast in the Blue Note one day. She was very stern. Those cool grey eyes that look straight through you. She told me that the man I was talking about was not Laredo. And I was never to mention his name again. Or I would be in trouble.'

They had reached a set of lights on the main avenue. The green light was in their favour, so Carlos interrupted his tale to hustle them across to the crowded sidewalk on the other side. 'Not far to go now.'

Without further ado, or any attempt to renew his tale, Carlos piloted them through a cluster of stalls and barrows laden with household goods and coloured fabrics. They came to a flight of steps in Calle Tarija. This led upwards to what Carlos described, in a jocular tone, as the accident-prone intersection of several streets, generally known as Plaza Gaston Velasco. Here the Blue Note was to be found.

He must have noticed that Ian was short of breath, an affliction familiar to those recently arrived in La Paz. 'Never mind the altitude.' He dug into the top pocket of his shirt and with a broad but mischievous grin handed Ian a business card. 'As the owner of the Bar says on his card: *the Blue Note serves the highest and driest martini in the world.* That'll soon fix you up. And if it doesn't, there'll probably be some coca leaves under the counter to take you to an even higher plane.'

They began to climb the steps, but slowly, pausing from time to time as Ian struggled to catch his breath. Among the myriad of signs and billboards overhanging the steps, spruiking everything from Coca Cola and Money Exchange to a floor show at the Tucan Bistro, Ian noticed a modest inscription saying simply Farmacia 24 Horas. Should he find his way to it and acquire some tablets for altitude sickness? He pushed the thought out of his mind. Instead, he took advantage of one of their pauses to renew his questioning.

'But in later years? Did you ever see or meet Laredo in the years after Che's campaign?'

'I can't be sure of that. But I doubt it. Since we left off driving for Canela, I haven't seen so much of the lady, apart from an occasional errand or a chat in a wine bar. Too busy tending to my own affairs. Keeping track of things. But you can be sure of this. With her journalistic background, she's always cruising around, close to what's happening. You never know whether the people she's mixing with are friends or acquaintances, or simply politicians she's been working on.'

While they paused for another breather, he summed up. 'As you must have gathered from Laredo's writings, she was also originally from Paraguay. They both had forebears from overseas. Australians in his case, Germans for her. She came from the settlement in Paraguay set up after the Franco-German war. Which probably explains her connection to German visitors over the years, like the archaeologists we took to Tiwanaku. And the way she keeps in touch with the Maestro.'

Carlos devoured the last of his nuts and screwed up the paper bag. He tossed the crumpled ball of paper at an overflowing rubbish bin as they pushed ahead. 'But I don't really know too much about her friends, or who she's been seeing over the years. I'm always polite when I see her, but I've kept my distance. Especially after she told me never to mention Laredo. To me that sounded like a threat. No need for Old Man Trouble at my door.'

Then he shrugged, and seemed to dismiss everything he had just been saying with a languid gesture. 'What more can I add? We are here in Latin America where writers and critics boast of our fanciful past. Jesuit missions and settlements of one kind or another are set up, then fade away. People come and go, fleeing from this or that, or starting over, re-inventing themselves, if that's what they have to do. Robert Leroy

Parker becomes Butch Cassidy and may or may not be buried at San Vincente. Che Guevara turns himself into a Uruguayan businessman and may or may not have been buried at Vallegrande. Re-buried later at a Cuban mausoleum, or so it is said. Marvic Laredo, according to his article, starts off in Paraguay as the boy soldier, *el Australiano*, then moves on to Buenos Aires and La Paz. He becomes eventually, I suppose, whoever he wants to be.'

On the landing at the top of the steps. Carlos felt obliged to round off his ruminations. 'So there it is. I know a little of what's happening in the back streets, but not so much about the halls of power in Plaza Murillo or Havana. I'm not much help when it comes to disentangling all those stories.'

'Because you can't rely on what people say? Or because you think some things are best left alone?'

Carlos shrugged. 'It could be either. The risks are always there. Who knows? One way or another, you'll have to look to Canela Dochera for your answers. But go carefully. She's always been very secretive. And she has powerful friends. I've gathered from my own dealings with her that there are many things she wants to keep to herself.'

This provoked another mischievous smile. 'According to my father, she not only hired his cars but on one occasion, a van. To take a dance troupe to the carnival at Oruro. While she was there, she always wore a mask, just like her dancers. You couldn't tell whether the performers in her troupe were men or women. You couldn't tell whether Canela, as the person in charge, was actually behind the mask she started out with, or whether she had passed it on to someone else. Not that it mattered. Oruro at carnival time is what it is: a whirl of masks and costumes and many mysteries, but principally a fiesta for *indigenas originarios*. Original peoples, as they like to call themselves. They'll clap and cheer everything, so long as it's both mystifying and lively. You can wear a zebra costume and they'll treat you like a donkey. You can act like a hyena and they'll call you a lion. You never know what's going to happen next — so long as the tambourines are jangling, the drums are beating, and the fire-crackers and cartouches are exploding.'

6

THE BLUE NOTE

They had reached Plaza Gaston Velasco. At last. Not so much a plaza – or so it seemed to Ian – as simply a crossways servicing various narrow thoroughfares: Calle Viluyo, Linares, Juan XXIII and the Tarija steps. It was apparent from a small sign on the far side that the entrance to the Blue Note was on the ground floor of a drab apartment block, the building's curved façade nosing into the street. A roller door coiled above the entrance to the bar, with heavy padlocks dangling from each end of the metal cylinder, was somewhat forbidding. It resembled other doors of that kind bunched above various workshops nearby, the areas within occupied by tool-benches, stacks of tyres and jumbles of jerry-cans. This was a district, the padlocks suggested, where buildings and shopfronts had to be locked up tightly at night.

Carlos led the way across the square. He stood aside as they reached the entrance to the bar, with the hint of a bow, as if to confirm that this was indeed their destination. Once inside, after pushing through the half-open portal, and edging down a small flight of wooden steps, Ian found himself in what seemed to be surprisingly congenial surroundings: a bar attended by a bearded figure, a backdrop of shelves filled with bottles of spirits and liqueurs, a large jar marked 'Tips' by the beer taps and a rack of Santa Ana wine bottles nearby. Further on, there were some alcoves furnished with tables and chairs, in the centre of each table a wax-encrusted wine bottle sealed with a burnt-out candle stub.

In one of the alcoves, there were a couple of drinkers talking quietly. A dishevelled fellow in a flannel suit was seated at the bar. Perched on a high stool, he was studying the playing cards in front of him, a game of Patience, presumably. One hand was on his glass of beer. Apart from these few, the place was devoid of customers. This was pleasing, and possibly why it had been chosen as a place to meet the lady. A private conversation could be had in one of the alcoves, with little risk, at this hour of the day, of being noticed.

Carlos gave a nod to the barman and found a seat for himself on the nearest bar stool. He invited Ian to join him by patting the neighbouring stool. That done, he pushed aside the jar for tips as if to clear the ground before introductions were effected. But the barman got in first, holding out a hand to Ian. 'Charlie Dean,' he declared. 'Carlos has probably told you about me already. Ginger beard and all. If he hasn't, he'll be lucky to get a drink.'

Carlos smiled patiently. 'Haven't had time for things like that. We've been talking about Butch Cassidy and the Sundance Kid.'

Charlie rolled his eyes. 'What can I say?' He flapped a hand at a the back of the room. 'No need to look. Your poster is in its usual place.'

This piece of jocular advice was ignored. Carlos leaned outwards to take in something on a wall just out of Ian's range of vision. 'True enough,' he confirmed. 'There it is, just as it should be.'

This was too much for the card player, 'Spare me all that nonsense. Some of us are here to have a quiet drink.'

'And so are we.' Carlos turned back to the bar and from his high stool at the centre of the premises, in a lordly manner, proceeded with his round of introductions. 'From Australia, Ian Thornton. Behind the bar, as previously confessed, Charlie Dean, a refugee from Toronto. And way up there, by the floodlit fridge bar full of warm beer and cans of coke, a local man, Senor Javier Facundas. Journalist, editor and broadcaster. And probably much else he won't admit to.'

The card player, overweight, perspiring, responded to this with a peevish look. 'No nonsense.' He took a sip of beer, wiping the froth away with the back of his hand. 'Isn't that what I just said? Some of us aren't in the mood for it.'

Carlos made a dismissive gesture. The two men obviously knew each other very well. While playing a familiar game, they could make the next move without much effort. 'No offence intended. We will leave you to potter about with your cards, and ponder your fate.'

Facundas loosened his tie. 'You should try pondering the column I wrote yesterday.'

'The same old thing, I expect.'

'The *main* thing. Who's running the Witches' Market? The Mayor or one of your crew? Butch Cassidy perhaps.' He finished with another jibe before turning back to his cards. 'Ponder that.'

Carlos pretended to laugh heartily at this, 'Whatever!' He leaned closer to Ian, enunciating his words carefully in a stage whisper. 'A tiny joke between us. When things go wrong he blames the gringos. The foreign interlopers. He reckons Butch Cassidy and the Sundance Kid were invented by the CIA. But I never argue. Just to annoy him. The CIA wasn't around at that time is all I say. Go watch the movie. What more can be said? That's Javier Facundas for you. A would-be investigative journalist of the old school. Watergate and all that. Spends his time watching power-plays in the Council chambers when he should be watching movies on TV. These days, I keep telling him, that's where the real power is. On the screen.'

'I heard most of that.' The journalist turned over another card without looking up. 'Facts matter.'

'I'll ponder that,' Carlos assured him, with a kind of chuckle.

'Whatever it means. Not much in this part of the world.'

Facundas raised an irritable hand like a policeman at a busy intersection trying to halt the flow of traffic. 'Don't start your magic realism rant. I've heard it all before. I've met your friend now. Let's leave it at that.'

Carlos nodded, pleasantly, but with the air of a man who has scored a point at his opponent's expense. 'Yes, we have said enough for one day. We will leave you in peace.'

These preliminaries now complete, Charlie, who had been waiting patiently for the toing and froing to end, took their orders. A few minutes later, the beer served, he placed his hands on the bar, and spoke to Ian directly, in a leisurely way. 'I'm from Toronto, true. But not just a refugee, or any of the other things our not-so-witty friend might say to stir things up. A traveller at first, then a writer, and much else. That's me. In addition to running the Blue Note. This is where travel writers can meet to swap stories. Work out where to go next.'

'Show him your latest book,' Carlos interposed. 'It's well worth reading, by all accounts. And bound to be of interest to Ian here. He's working with Kurt Meissner at the Chiquitos missions.'

'The Maestro!' Charlie uttered the name in a reverent tone. 'You're a lucky man. He knows so much. And he had some fine things to say about my book. I have a section on the Choro trail which starts at Cumbre, on the way out of La Paz, and runs on across the mountains to Coroico. The various displaced people in that area. Which is why I needed the Maestro's help for background. The Afro-Bolivian community at Tocana, for example. Mostly oppressed workers from the mines at Potosi. They founded their own township in the 1950s, after the revolution. They converse in Aymaran and wear *cholita* clothing, but they keep their African traditions. Fiestas in the Senegal style.'

He fossicked under the counter and brought up a copy of his book, the cover dominated by a mountainous landscape. 'Charobamba also.' He opened the book at some photographs of men and women in ragged garments, standing by tiny huts, mules in pens nearby. 'A village founded by Jews. Exiles from Germany in the 1930s. They reconnected to Sephardic Jews expelled from Spain in the 16th century, according to the Maestro. Which is why some of them speak Ladino, derived from mediaeval Spanish. Although he told me to keep that out of my book, as it might be thought too far-fetched. An overdose of 'magic realism', the phrase so often used by travel writers these days.'

Carlos had been listening to all of this with a good-natured but condescending smile. 'And by the Maestro too. Magic realism! It will soon be used to sell you 50 copies of this little book, if you don't watch out.' With another smile, the Maestro's cynical agent pushed the book aside. 'So let me change the subject before it's too late. We have more important things to think about.' He leaned closer to the man behind the bar. 'We are here to meet the lady.'

Charlie fingered his ginger beard. 'Ingrid or Canela?' he inquired, cautiously.

This was greeted with a frown. 'Ingrid is the one I spoke to, because she's the one who always comes to the door. Made me wait, as usual, but when she came back, she said the lady would come to the Blue Note this morning. So the question is: any sign of her? Or either of them?'

Carlos twisted in his seat to add a few words of explanation for Ian's benefit. 'Ingrid Kahn is the lady's niece. Her brother's daughter from a second marriage. She came to La Paz from Paraguay some years ago, to keep her aunt company. Quite attractive, but not as young as she once was. Keeps the household running while her aunt is out and about, flattering politicians and pulling strings.'

'Keeps the household running for the two of them,' Charlie Dean chipped in. 'While her aunt keeps the Witches' Market running for those who can pay the price.'

Javier Facundas, pretending to study his cards, was listening in.

'There are others in that household,' he observed. 'Not just the two women. One other at least.'

Carlos was quick to cut short this intervention. 'We aren't here to talk about housekeeping. My task was to get a message to the woman I've known since boyhood. Arrange a meeting. And that I've done.'

'Well, there's no sign of the dragon lady yet.' Charlie had returned his unwanted book to its place beneath the bar. 'I'm hoping she'll send Ingrid instead. That's what happened when that American fellow came snooping around. Looking for stuff about Che's campaign and so on. Anyone with something to say before the 50th anniversary in Cuba gets going. He was hoping to quiz the lady herself.'

'I wasn't in on that.' Carlos spoke defensively. 'The American went about it in the wrong way. Ruffled feathers. This is different. A nice polite approach by an old friend. On behalf of the Maestro. Ingrid told me Canela would come, and I'm sure she will.'

'Have it your own way.' Charlie topped up their glasses. 'There's plenty of time.'

Carlos was about to say something in answer to this, when there was a movement at the top of the stairs. A dark form in silhouette had appeared in the doorway, feminine, the facial expression hard to make out against the glare from outside. She moved inwards, parting the strands of beads marking the entrance to the bar, descending quietly and gracefully. A woman in a close-fitting skirt and a denim jacket. She took in the scene before her with a slightly bewildered gaze.

'Ingrid,' Carlos informed Ian in a whispered aside. 'The lady's niece. Which is not what I wanted. They make their promises, then please themselves. So be it. We've done well to get at least one of them here.'

'But will she be able to tell us anything about Laredo if she's only been in La Paz for a few years?'

'She comes from Paraguay, like her aunt. And as Laredo did. Or so they say. That could be useful.'

Carlos left his stool to greet the newcomer with a clumsy bow. 'What a pleasure. So extremely good to see you.'

His awkward greeting brought her to a sudden halt. She gripped the handrail for support. A gentle soul, Ian concluded, good-looking in a quiet way, with auburn hair and a neat figure, but ill-at-ease. Not really the sort of person to please herself.

She had come alone, he surmised, not because she was in the habit of pleasing herself as Carlos had implied, but under instruction from her elderly and domineering aunt, a 'dragon lady' according to the tittle-tattle that had just taken place. Those around Ian in the bar, it seemed, were capable of slandering her by adding a dash of rouge to her reputation, then suggesting that her painted features had been ruined by magic realism or some other literary trick.

He would have to watch all of them closely.

Ingrid was still looking unsure of herself, but she must have sensed that Ian, the stranger in the group, was the best person to speak to, the one most likely to heed the message she had been instructed to bring. She spoke to him directly, in a quiet tone: 'I am here for my aunt.'

As Ian rose from his place by the bar, she stepped towards him. 'My aunt would have wanted to be here herself. But that proved impossible. She is indisposed. You will accept her apology, I trust.'

'Of course.' There was something irresistible in her formal manner which prompted Ian to nod quietly and make a small bow of his own, which she seemed to appreciate.

But Carlos couldn't suppress his annoyance. 'First the American. And now another apology!' He shook her outstretched hand abruptly. 'It seems we will have to accept this. I trust she tried very hard to be here. As promised.'

'These things happen.'

Her sweet reply failed to appease him. With a gleam in his eye, the Maestro's agent added a footnote to their exchanges. 'She is being pestered by the American, or so we've heard. A scholar of some sort, he says. If that's what he actually is. Your mistress is worn down by busybodies, perhaps. Not inclined to talk about times past at present.'

His inquisitive tone was not to her liking. 'I know nothing of that. And she's not my mistress, she's my aunt. She will speak for herself as to what can be discussed. I was told to say she was indisposed, and that's what I have done.'

It looked as though she might now simply back off and leave, so Carlos quickly gave up any further attempt to extract a more fulsome apology, or to gather information about the American. His frown became a smile, but only just. He proceeded to introduce Ian, mentioning his background in archaeology and his work with the Maestro at the Chiquitos missions. In the course of this presentation, he began shepherding Ian and Ingrid, the two visitors, towards an alcove on the far side of the room. This, presumably, was to keep anything talked about well away from Charlie Dean and Javier Facundas, although, outwardly, the barman was busy wiping his beer taps with a cloth and the journalist still seemed focused on his card game.

Carlos remained standing as they took their seats on opposite sides of a table in the alcove. 'You must stay for a little while at least,' he counselled Ingrid. 'You will recall from our conversation yesterday that my friend Senor Thornton has an interest in the life and times of your aunt's former comrade, Marvic Laredo. One of Che's finest heroes. With him to the very end, apparently. I feel sure you will hear what our friend has to say and pass it on. It's all in a good cause, I am led to believe. A boost to Che's admirers in Australia, including our friend's sister. She is seeking to honour Che and his comrades in a magnificent work of art. No harm in that, of course. Good news, in fact.' He smiled mischievously. 'It will lift your aunt's spirits when she hears about that. Put her on the path to a full recovery, eh?'

Ingrid stared at him impassively. 'I'll pass on what is necessary. So long as it's not disturbing. We lead a quiet life in our house. The two of us. The past is a closed book, as my aunt is often heard to say.'

'Can I get you something to drink?' Her tone had quashed his pretence of jocularity. 'Anything you like.'

'There's no need for that. I won't be staying long.'

'Then I'll leave you in peace.' Carlos backed out of the alcove with the air of a waiter whose dignity has been affronted.

Ingrid turned back to Ian, smiling faintly, her blue-eyed gaze upon him surprisingly trusting. She brought her hands together and rested her arms on the table in a relaxed way, as though both she and Ian were of one mind: pleased to be rid of an inconvenient third party. 'I'm always wary of Carlos Quirigo. And so is my aunt. He claims to be a great friend of our household, but we always keep him at arm's length. His father had a close connection. Way back. But Carlos makes too much of that.'

There was no time to lose, so Ian went straight to the vital question. 'Will you speak to your aunt on my behalf? I would very much like to meet her. For the various reasons you've already heard about.'

'You must tell me a little more.' Her tone was sympathetic, but her unwavering expression hard to construe. 'You must tell me more about yourself, and about your sister. They are not always so easy to deal with, these artists and writers. Their plans and ideas so often up in the air, while others with their feet on the ground are left to do the work.' She glanced at her watch. 'I can only spare you a few minutes – or my no-nonsense aunt will be wanting to know where I've been. And why I've taken so long.'

There was now a note of impatience in her tone. It seemed to Ian that this probably had more to do with the way in which her aunt controlled the household than with the request he had just made. Ingrid may well have sensed that they were both being pushed and pulled by the whims of others, and would prefer to be doing something else. If this were so, she could possibly be won over by hearing more about his sister than he might otherwise have mentioned. So he began with a short overview of Anita's life as an artist and the art collective she was working with in Sydney. He moved on to Anita's belief that Laredo's links to the Australian settlers in Paraguay, and to his role in Che's campaign, could be of use in the art prize she hoped to win.

Ingrid listened quietly. She asked some questions along the way, and her gaze softened as she did so, especially when Ian faltered in trying to set out clearly, or at least in a way that could be readily understood, what his sister's work of art might look like.

Towards the end of his description, Ingrid nodded, as though she knew from personal experience how difficult it was to fathom the odd ideas of artists and writers. When he went on to speak of the Australian settlement in Paraguay, she straightened up and listened keenly, making some remarks in passing about her childhood and the challenges generally faced by migrant groups in that country.

Her family, the Kahn's were amongst the earliest settlers in the German colony, she informed him, but when her aunt married into a local family by the name of Cochera, it didn't work out. Canela was too German to fit into a family of Spanish descent. Which was why she took off to become a journalist in Buenos Aires, then La Paz, before any children arrived.

'I am supposed to be a kind of daughter,' she continued, with a weary smile. 'But I often feel more like a maid in my aunt's fine old house, always at another's beck and call. As it may have been for you in making these enquiries. But my father won't hear a word against his sister, so I've stayed on. Canela Dochera is very well-known, he always says. Widely respected in La Paz and elsewhere. But, like all the Kahns, he probably says such a thing because he and sister have always been of use to each other. Exchanging favours when it suits them.'

Apart from a few observations of this kind, Ian's companion in the alcove had given little away as to what she and her aunt might know about Che Guevara or Marvic Laredo. Nonetheless, the conversation seemed to have reached a reasonably comfortable stage, a moment to bring it back to his opening question. The indications were that the two of them shared an understanding of the ways in which family members could achieve their aims by playing on the affections of those around them. The time had come to settle things.

'You've taken an interest in what I've said,' Ian commenced. 'For which I thank you. But let me add this. I gather from what I've heard that Marvic Laredo was a close friend of your aunt. It is only she who can tell me what I need to know. His whereabouts. Or whether she has any diaries or papers belonging to him. Papers revealing what we need to know. So let me ask you this, directly, but with respect: can she be persuaded to meet me?'

'She is indisposed.'

'So you've said. But only for today perhaps. To spend a short time with her on my sister's behalf seems such a small thing to ask. An art competition in a distant country. And the matters in question so long ago.'

Ingrid leaned forward, hands clasped tightly now. 'There is more in this than you realise,' she whispered. 'Far more. With reputations at stake, and much else at risk of ending up in flames. That could happen if the past that should be kept safely closed is opened up. Especially with the 50th anniversary of Che's death approaching.'

'But Laredo's role – all of that. Everything happened so long ago?'

A small frown and a glance at the nearest window was enough to make her disagreement clear. 'The past is always here. Walk the streets outside. You'll see Che's picture on many walls. His face on the placards in Plaza Murillo. Hoisted high in every protest. He is with us still and he always will be. He lives.'

'Of course. But simply as an image. Not in reality.'

She laughed at this. 'Reality is always changing. Che is out and about. All over. In the next street and far afield. Above and below ground. On T-shirts, TV screens and airwaves. He is everywhere. But what he was really like, and what his comrades thought of him, that is not for me to say. I am not old enough to know it all.'

Now it was Ian's turn to close the gap, trying not to be too insistent as he leaned towards her, but knowing that this might be his only chance to get what he wanted. 'Can you persuade your aunt to meet me?'

'I doubt it. She knows how one thing can lead to another. You have seen the statue of President Villaroel? That sculpted image beneath a street lamp in Plaza Murillo?'

'I have.'

'My aunt knows people who were there when a mob dragged Villaroel out of his chambers and hanged him from that lamp. All of this in the aftermath of the Chaco war. Some years after the Armistice, but close enough in time to matter. The past returns, so often unexpectedly. It comes back to haunt those who had hoped it had been forgotten.'

She was speaking vehemently, but with a strangely distracted air. It struck Ian that she probably spent too much time alone with her thoughts, obliged to echo what she heard from her aunt, probably in an oft-repeated form, but at the same time trying to make sense of it herself.

When he had spoken of his family, and the way in which Anita had been deprived of her mother while still a teenager, leaving the aspiring artist with a cluster of increasingly obsessive ideas, Ingrid had seemed to grasp immediately what lay behind his unusual quest. *Always at another's beck and call.* She had not only linked what he had said to her own experience, her dealings with a wilful aunt, but also to certain blind spots shared by her aunt and Ian's sister, fixations that could be seen as frailties. This shared perception, Ian realised, had created a bond of sorts.

But Ingrid, after seeming, momentarily, to recognise what they had in common, was now breaking away from him, brought back to the reality of the Witches' Market, disturbed by more than family flaws.

'Che's campaign was not so long ago,' she declared. 'Far from it. Do you think Fidel Castro and his comrades in Havana wish to be reminded of allegations that they abandoned Che? Left him in the wilds of Bolivia without assistance, as Laredo might say? Or may have said already in his writings, if further papers come to light? Will leading figures in Bolivia, or their sons and daughters, appreciate disclosures that Che's defeat was brought about by machinations of the CIA? That in the end Che's force was weakened by deceptions and betrayals? That steps were taken to procure his defeat, leaving questions to be answered as to who was involved? Or who has to be silenced to prevent the true story being spread everywhere?'

Ingrid took a deep breath and sat back. 'You are here for your sister. I can follow why that is, and why it seems, from so far away, that details don't really matter. But you will have gathered, from what I've told you, there is more than art mixed up in all of this. My aunt has moved from one country to another, from one place to the next, and in each place she fits in by using camouflage. She learnt that lesson early on, she told me, from the ingenious wordsmiths at Café Tortoni in Buenos Aires. And again when she reached La Paz. Wear a mask. It was the same when she wrote for the broadsheet called *Amauta*. It means 'Wise Teacher' in Quechua. Keep your real feelings to yourself. That was the wisdom she took to heart. And that is what she has always done. That piece of wisdom is with her still.'

Ian leaned even closer. 'I hear everything you say. But you have to help me.'

She sighed, and looked around wildly, as if fearing that anything she said might be overheard. She paused for a moment before framing her reply. 'You are very persuasive. Which is probably because we understand each other. I would like to be of use to you. But now I must leave.'

'Thank you.' Ian touched her hand. 'Whichever way it goes, I would like to see you again. I've enjoyed our conversation.'

She was flustered by this, but seemed pleased. Her manner softened a little. 'Yes, your tale, and your sister's wish to create something special, is very persuasive. You have opened up some new vistas for me.'

Then, conscious that she might have said too much, she quickly rose to her feet. 'I must leave. I'll contact you if I can be of use. At your hotel, or through Carlos. But do not hope for too much.'

He watched her stride briskly to the small flight of steps and grip the handrail. Carlos, simultaneously, left his stool at the bar. 'Let me help you to the door.' He was clearly determined to follow her and have a last word before she disappeared.

As the two of them made their way into the street, Ian edged towards the bar, and placed his empty glass on one of the beer mats. He was about to mount the steps himself when he was suddenly accosted by Javier Facundas. The dishevelled journalist had abandoned his cards to snatch at Ian's sleeve in a furtive way.

'Be careful,' Facundas warned. 'You can't trust Ingrid Kahn, and you certainly can't trust that old schemer, Canela Dochera. She's always been a power behind the scenes in this city, and she still is. Not only in the Witches' Market, but in the corridors and offices around Plaza Murillo.'

He drew closer. 'If you get to ask any questions of the lady, include one about who exactly is living in their house. They pretend it's just the two of them, but I have information to the contrary. Will Canela talk to you? She'll do her best to avoid a meeting. Because she and Marvic Laredo are the only ones who really know what happened in the ambush that ended Che's campaign. Only they know whether he was buried at Vallegrande. And all of that will bring you to the vital question: whether

Che was betrayed and, if so, by whom? These are the hard questions that have to be asked. They're the questions to which everyone returns. They can be used to arouse a mob in the streets, even now.'

Ian groped for the nearest bar stool and slowly eased himself into the seat. 'You seem to know a lot. About facts and matters that could be useful to me.' He paused to let this thought sink in, then put it to Facundas squarely. 'I'd like to hear a little more of what you have to say. To sort out fact and fiction. Let's meet again.'

7

A MEETING AT VARINO

A meeting with Javier Facundas for a longer talk about Ingrid and her aunt was arranged quickly, before Carlos reappeared. The Maestro's agent had been helpful in setting up a meeting at the Blue Note, but his breezy manner and indiscreet comments, plus his clumsy offer to help Ingrid up the steps as she left the wine bar, had made it clear to Ian that he should seek further information on his own.

The Hotel Varino was a good place to meet, Facundas agreed. This suited Ian. The Varino was close to Plaza Murillo, and only a few streets away from Ian's hotel. He could well remember having lunch with the Maestro at the café in the Varino courtyard when he had first arrived in La Paz, a congenial way of getting to know the elderly German scholar. Concealed from passers-by in the street by an archway entrance, this was the right place for a quiet talk.

Ian made no mention of his earlier visit to the Varino when he found Facundas seated at a small marble-topped table in the courtyard on the day after their brief encounter at the Blue Note. He didn't want to give too much away. Rather, he had to find out what Facundas knew.

The local journalist proved willing to talk at greater length about Canela Dochera and her niece. With a beer in front of him, he was soon adding more to the cryptic comments he had made in passing at the Blue Note, checking details in his notebook as he talked.

The information he was keen to pass on was fascinating, but hard to fathom. What he said about Canela Dochera's role in Che's final campaign, and whether there were any papers in her possession concerning Marvic Laredo, raised a host of further questions. It seemed from what Facundas claimed to know about Laredo and his friends that Che's heroic reputation was at risk. In some corners of La Paz, Facundas hinted, both then and now, Che's attempt to ferment widespread revolution in Bolivia and neighbouring countries was thought to be foolhardy and a cause of needless grief.

Speaking softly, glancing at adjoining tables in the courtyard as if wary of the café's other customers, the journalist drew mainly on his recent get-together with the American scholar who was close to finishing a piece about Che's ill-fated campaign. Now and again, as if to substantiate the details he had been given, Facundas pointed to an entry in his little book, a note of what he had been told.

The American, Dan Brady, a Professorial Fellow attached to Skidmore College in upstate New York, had been aiming to contact a number of Che's former comrades. While in Havana, apparently, Brady had come across Laredo's documents, the article and the unpublished draft. This had led to wider correspondence. He had sent letters to Che's contemporaries in Argentina and to Tania's relatives in Germany. He had sought information from people who were thought to have been present at Vallegrande after the final battle, and from those who may have encountered the remnants of Che's force on their journey back to Cuba via Santiago, Sydney and Prague.

Brady had then decided to visit some of the places mentioned in Laredo's article, such as Che's recruitment camp in Cuba and Café Tortino in Buenos Aires. On his way to La Paz, he stopped off at Asuncion in Paraguay to find out what remained of the former Australian colony where some of the boy soldiers in the Chaco war were said to have been brought up, according to newspapers covering the conflict.

Brady's enquiries established that after disembarking at Ascuncion on the Rio Paraguay in the 1890s, the Australian settlers had set forth with all their belongings piled on *carreta* oxcarts. They pushed ahead slowly and with great difficulty to reach the land allotted to them, further north at a place called Cosme. This was to be the site of their enlightened egalitarian community.

The Australians had worked hard to carve out a viable settlement at Cosme, but it wasn't long before people started to fall out, due to differing opinions as to what should be done. Arguments and conflict had led to a loss of cohesion, a fracturing of the group. Rival communities were set up in other localities.

Brady hired a car in Ascunion and set off for Cosme with a local driver who knew the way. The roads were in bad condition, and some of them, towards the end of the trip, were scarcely more than muddy tracks, churned-up ruts, probably much like the tracks taken by the Australian settlers in the 19th century. The car seemed constantly at risk of sliding into the undergrowth or the nearest ditch. But his driver kept saying it was always bad at this time of year, and kept going. Eventually, they reached Cosme.

According to Brady, the original settlement turned out to be little more than a cluster of meagre dwellings, some with thatched roofs. A number of them looked like sheds attached to a deserted railway siding. There was an old homestead flanked by a couple of palm trees, its timbers collapsing under the burden of a rusting iron roof and with vines pushing through holes in its walls. The wide streets nearby – a ghostly tribute to the original Utopian dream – were not only empty but overgrown with weeds and grass, save for a few ruts here and there scarred red by *carreta* wheels.

With the driver's help, Brady asked around. They finished up sitting with some inhabitants of the derelict township, sipping *yerbe maté*. Yes, the locals acknowledged, some of them had Australian ancestors, but none of them had heard of a family called Laredo. Of course, all those with memories of the original colony had passed on, and most of their children were living elsewhere.

Brady and his driver were taken to the local church, but there was no mention of a family called Laredo in its records. On a walk to the old cemetery they were shown a weathered fence-post made from *lapacho* wood which was said to be the last one left from the days of the original colony. They were shown some graves in the cemetery, most of them obscured by brambles, many lacking headstones. The names they located were of no significance.

On the way back to their car, the driver noticed a forgotten half-torn circus poster on a cement wall, showing a cartoon picture of a kangaroo in boxing gloves, shaping up to an invisible foe. *El Circo del Canguro Boxeador*, the words on the poster said. This amused the driver. '*Muy bien!*' he exclaimed. 'A boxing kangaroo! *El Australiano, eh?*' Brady took a photo of it to please his companion. He was well aware that the image, like the stones in the cemetery, added nothing much to his research.

The villagers stood in the doorways of their little houses and waited for the car to leave. Brady waved farewell, but they didn't wave back. The story of the original dream was lost to them, it seemed, perhaps because it was a reminder of defeat. When he asked the driver whether that might be so, the man answered with a Spanish phrase that ruled a sombre line beneath their quest: *No me molestes con hablar más de los viejos tiempos. Don't bother me with any more talk of old times.*

It was getting dark, it had started to rain, and the car was hard to handle. '*Si me muero, que me muero,*' the driver added. '*If I die, let me die.* That's enough for me.' He wouldn't say more, hands on the steering wheel, his gaze fixed on the slippery track ahead.

A few days later, back in Ascuncion, while in the local archives trawling through registers of births, deaths and marriages, Brady found the name Laredo scattered here and there, with some addresses in the vicinity of Cosme. But he couldn't turn up a certificate or any other record, not even in a newspaper, verifying the birth of Marvic Blas Laredo. Articles about the Chaco war mentioned boy soldiers, one of whom was known as *el Australiano,* but his actual name was not provided.

It was after these rather fruitless efforts that the American had moved on to La Paz. He had been hoping to interview Canela Dochera, even though he was well aware that since she had failed to answer his letters, this would be difficult.

And so it had proved to be, Facundas informed Ian, glancing around the Varino courtyard, before turning back to his notebook and the next phase of Brady's research.

Unwisely, without pausing to contrive an introduction, the American had taken a deep breath and gone straight to Canela's door. Somehow or other, by sheer persistence perhaps, he prevailed upon the niece to admit him and to present his card: Professor Dan Brady. Within a very short time, Ingrid reappeared with the lady herself. The uninvited Professor (*an American gringo,* she called him to his face) was given short shrift. He was told to leave.

Having brought his narrative to this point, Facundas leaned closer to Ian with an air of increasing excitement. He pointed to a passage in his notes recording what Brady had called 'a crucial moment'.

While standing in the front hall of the Cochera residence, waiting for the lady to appear, Brady had taken it upon himself to peer quickly into an adjoining room. He glimpsed an elderly man in a wheelchair seated in front of a TV set, a rug draped across his knees. The man's back was to the door and his face could not be seen. He seemed to be talking to himself, or perhaps to the TV screen.

Brady was caught in the doorway by the lady herself. She was moving towards him fast, and was clearly indignant. She slammed shut the door to the TV room. Then turned and denounced Brady as a trespasser. Any hope of talking to her was gone.

Brady deduced that she was determined to conceal not only the presence of a third person on the premises, but also the identity of the man in the wheelchair. Her speedy, furtive action, in the presence of a researcher she knew had come to La Paz from Cosme, and who was known to be looking for one of Che's comrades with a link to Paraguay, strongly suggested that Brady had caught a glimpse of Marvic Blas Laredo.

Javier Facundas closed his notebook. He had questioned Brady closely, he assured Ian, and was inclined to agree that the man in the TV room probably was Laredo. A quick sip of beer brought Facundas to another point. He reminded Ian of Ingrid Kahn's evasiveness. Hadn't she told Ian at the Blue Note that the Dochera household consisted of two people only: the lady and Ingrid herself? When he heard her say that, Facundas realised he had to meet Ian and share what he knew.

So what was the solution to the Laredo mystery? If Ian did manage to secure a meeting with Canela Dochera he should be ready to press her about the identity of the third person in her house. This would help to clear up the Laredo conundrum once and for all. There could be something in such a solution for each of them.

Ian had been listening intently. Facundas' desire to forge a mutually beneficial outcome was understandable, but it was undercut by what he said next. Ian had made it clear, while arranging to meet at the Varino, that his task was to sort out what was real and what was illusory about the Laredo story, and also who could be trusted to tell it. Facundas must have forgotten this. He seemed to assume that Ian knew as much about the back street lore of La Paz as Facundas did, and the way in which its stories could be slanted or embellished.

'Take Carlos Quirigo!' Facundas uttered the name in a sardonic tone, as if he were adding a small but probably unnecessary footnote to the tale he had just told. 'Carlos doesn't believe what I say about the man in the wheelchair. He doesn't think he's Laredo. He claims to have caught a glimpse of him on one occasion while talking to Ingrid at the door. The man he saw in front of TV, according to Carlos, was one of the drivers in his father's fleet. He was injured in an accident while driving for Canela, and was an occasional visitor to the house *for old times' sake.*'

Facundas gave a faint snort 'His father's so-called *fleet*. What is one to believe about anything thrown into the ring by Carlos Quirigo? He brags about his Butch Cassidy posters, but the truth is he stole the idea from his friend at the Camino Hotel. A friend who had been taking tourists to the San Vincente shoot-out scene for years, until Carlos moved in to swell his own wallet with tourist dollars.'

'Those posters!' Facundas snorted derisively again. 'Dan Brady told me that, in the course of his usual spiel about Butch Cassidy, our man Carlos claimed his poster at the Hotel Mundus Novus was removed amicably, because a new manager had done his own research about the gringo bandits. What rubbish! The manager ripped it up after Carlos pleasured a hooker in the Honeymoon Suite for several days, then tried to sneak out without paying the bill. Carlos Quirigo! He learnt half his tricks while driving for his father, and the other half working for a security firm in Cochabamba. They sent him to Miami for special training and to improve his English. But he spent most of his time in gambling dens run by anti-Castro Cuban expatriates, some of whom were said to be mixed up in protection rackets and assassinations. Which is where he probably learnt a few more tricks.'

It was at this point that Ian felt obliged to intervene. 'The Maestro seems to trust him.'

This halted the flow of ant-Carlos information, but the journalist's stance was far from reassuring. 'He trusts him for minor jobs, like putting you in touch with Canela's niece. But where the Maestro sits in all of this is a tale for another day. Right now, the important thing is to ignore what Carlos says about the man in the wheelchair. We can safely surmise that he's Marvic Laredo. And if he is, we can work together to find out what he knows and how we can use it.'

8

FIGURES ON THE DANCE FLOOR

What Facundas had told him was all very well, Ian murmured to himself after their talk. But was it of any real use to him? In reporting back to Anita in Sydney, what could he say about meeting Facundas with any real hope of raising her spirits?

The Brady/Facundas findings were ambiguous. There was no other word for it. There was no evidence of Laredo's birth in Paraguay, and doubts about his connection, if any, to the Australian colony at Cosme. The notion that Che's former comrade, author of the article sent to Anita from Havana, might still be alive seemed too far-fetched to be repeated. It was based on little more than a glimpse of an elderly fellow in a wheelchair. Moreover, there were indications that increasing speculation about Laredo and his writings could be used to cast doubt on Che's reputation, the status of which was central to Anita's project.

There were just too many doubts surrounding 'Laredo's life and times. Further, was it likely that the trustees of the Art Gallery in Sydney would be interested in the exploits of such a man? What significance would a tribute to Australian society based on the image of a freedom fighter in a faraway place have in modern Sydney?

Ian's recent email exchanges with Anita had been frustrating. They hadn't settled anything. Nonetheless, she probably had to be told, plainly and firmly, before she wasted more time, that her project wasn't worth pursuing. It was only he, as her brother, who could say what had to be said. Her friends in the art collective, and especially her particular friend, Kim Guest, were unlikely to be honest with her, for they seemed to be in the business of encouraging any old weird endeavour in the name of art.

So what should he say to Anita in his next email?

It was while these troubling thoughts were running through his mind that he received a pleasant message. The Maestro was on his way to La Paz to confer with a delegation from UNESCO on his work at the Chiquitos missions. He proved agreeable to a meeting and, once more, the courtyard café at the Varino was chosen as a convenient location. They could probably cover what had to be discussed during a lunch break, before the Maestro went back to his delegation.

On this occasion, Ian was placed at a table near the service area of the café, the centre of action from which a team of waiters kept coming and going, neatly attired in white shirts and bow-ties, like subalterns in a command post attending to incoming signals and quietly-whispered orders.

Ian felt uneasy. This was probably due to worries arising from his recent meeting with Facundas, his would-be fellow sleuth. He looked around. There was no sign of the Maestro. He ordered a glass of wine, pondering his next move and wondering what sort of advice he should seek from his colleague.

But he was gradually distracted by what was happening in front of him. On the far side of the courtyard, there was a small dance floor. The waiters began moving tables away from it while a group of musicians assembled on an elevated platform at one end, taking their places on the little bandstand. These preparations reminded Ian that on the way in he had noticed a poster declaring that a 'tango lunch' was held here on Saturdays and Sundays.

It wasn't long before the music started up and some couples, mostly middle-aged, made their way to the dance floor, responding to what was being played in a grave and carefully-practised manner. Coloured lights on strings across the courtyard had been turned on. These baubles in mid-air, as if floating in space above the marble-topped tables, lent the dance floor an other-worldly appearance, theatrical, but with a timeless aura, a setting that could be used for music-hall reminders of the past or a cabaret artist's skit about the future.

The musicians on the little bandstand were elderly fellows, several portly, one entirely bald. Their instruments looked as though they had been kept in old-fashioned vinyl cases from one era to the next. There was a bulky accordion, a couple of fiddles, an electric guitar with an oddly-shaped power-board attached to it and a keyboard on a metal trolley, manned by a player on a spindly stool.

The undemonstrative style of the musicians, and the way they played their instruments, seemed to fit the nature of the music itself. So did the movements and impassive features of the dancers. The hesitant shifts and changes in the tango rhythm, the unexpected pauses, the abrupt changes of direction, the see-sawing of the male and female bodies: all of these seemed reminiscent of some other age, a bygone world perhaps, as though Ian and those at the tables around him were being presented with scenes from a performance of many years ago. The figures on the dance floor, arms held stiffly, elbows out, sashayed to and fro like marionettes on a brightly-lit stage.

He was absorbed by the dancers, enchanted by the spectacle. But there was no way of losing himself entirely in the scene playing before him. He couldn't push his dilemma to one side.

The doubts he had expressed in his last email to Anita had failed to impress her. If anything, they had simply complicated the situation between them. He had emphasised the difficulty, even the futility of trying to get to the bottom of the Laredo mystery in the face of so much contradictory evidence. He had tried to talk her out of proceeding further by suggesting there were sources of inspiration closer to home she could draw upon as she cast about for a compelling theme or image. Surely there were sources related to her own personal experience, or experiences with a more striking Australian flavour? Surely these would be of greater interest to the trustees of the Gallery?

He had even reminded her of the day in her early years at art school when he had taken her to the Gallery to see the portraits entered for that year's Archibald Prize.

He had smiled remembering it while composing his email to her. It had proved to be an enjoyable outing, one of the few occasions, in the years before he left for his further studies at Harvard, when they had found time to spend together.

He had seen it as an opportunity to share a piece of family history that had been passed to him by his father. He had chosen his words carefully to summarise what his father had said, doing his best not to make too much of this distant, but still vivid memory, touching on it lightly. In his email he reminded her that after taking in the Archibald exhibition, they had returned to the front steps of the Gallery. Standing there, beneath the array of great artists emblazoned on the façade of the sandstone building, they had taken in the scene before them. A scattering of picnicking families were spread about the vast lawns of the Domain, with couples strolling to and fro in the shade provided by the dark green foliage of the Moreton Bay fig trees overhanging the approach to the Gallery.

He had realised that this was the moment to show Anita where his father had taken him as a boy. It was in this spot, according to his father, that something of real value was to be found.

His father's words had remained with him. They were in his thoughts as he and Anita made their way to the footpath beneath the line of giant trees, and eventually to a stalwart at the end of the row, slightly to one side of its picturesque companions.

In the gloom engendered by the heavy foliage, on a small lichen-covered stone lodged within the twisted, above-ground roots of the majestic tree, the words so important to his father and family were still faintly visible:

This spot marks the position of the Anzac buffet where during the years 1916 to 1920 82,000 soldiers and sailors were welcomed back on their return from the Great War. Erected by the members of the Mosman No. 8 Red Cross Voluntary Aides.

Anita had stood there beside him, listening quietly and attentively, in the manner of a youthful art student, as he told her the story: how his father's mother and her two sisters had been amongst those serving at the Red Cross buffet. Later, they and some of their fellow Aides had played a part in the creation and positioning of this stone. So this place was important to the Thornton family. It was an acute reminder of a small but poignant moment in time, inconsequential perhaps when measured against so many other greater moments and more enduring public structures, including the Art Gallery they had just visited, but significant in its own way.

The Voluntary Aides, according to his father, had always harboured a wry belief that, because their memorial, this 'Mosman stone', was small and unobtrusive, and embraced so firmly by the roots of the massive tree, it would probably never be moved or disposed of. Unlike so many monuments and public buildings, structures that all too often were demolished or ignored, succumbing to the restless mood of later generations, the 'Mosman stone' would always be there, a tiny but tangible presence.

In the course of his email about their visit to the 'Mosman stone', Ian had mentioned that he had written a number of poems after his father's death, recalling moments of this kind. Other moments he could still share by simply taking down a book from the shelves accommodating what remained of his father's library.

Reaching for a book on the library shelves, and opening it up, he would seem to share the feelings of the original owner. There was a sense of anticipation as to what the pages might reveal. He felt their connection to all the books nearby, and to other books and works of art in times past. At such a shared moment, one was never alone and never adrift.

These ruminations were meant not only as a reminder of their visit to the Art Gallery, a quiet moment they had shared, but also as a footnote to his gentle suggestion that creative works, books, paintings, sculpted images, could be drawn from personal experiences closer to home. Surely it wasn't necessary to seek acclaim for an obscure soldier in a distant country, such as Marvic Blas Laredo in Bolivia – especially when it was proving so difficult to find out anything much about him or to assess his worth.

What had been unwise, Ian now realised, with the benefit of hindsight, was the suggestion that there was another, less tangled way of her achieving success in the art world.

His aim had been to make it plain that whatever had happened on the futile quest for Laredo, he was on her side.

How wrong he had been. The match that had ignited Anita's scorching reply, he realised, was the reference he had made to the poem he had written about his father's library. She had been affronted. Was he the only one who could communicate with deeper feelings in this way?

Ian felt in his pocket for her email, which he had printed out to ponder carefully before replying. Slowly, and somewhat painfully, as the music from the players on the bandstand drifted by, he worked his way through it, sentence by sentence.

How can you be so insensitive? As if I could be expected to remember staring at some old stone outside the Art Gallery. Why would I even be interested? He was your father, not mine. The Women serving tea and scones at some long-ago Anzac buffet on the Domain have nothing to do with me. Your grandmother, not mine. But the worst thing about your email, as my good friend at our art collective pointed out, is the patronising way in which you're trying to distract me from my hunt for an image that matters. It might even serve your agenda to call up bits and pieces of the Anzac fantasy.

According to Kim's research, the prize I'm going for references a prize that was offered soon after the Art Gallery was built. The winner was an Australian artist called Dohra Ohlfsen, who was well-known for a series of medals commemorating Anzac soldiers. She was commissioned to design a bronze panel in a classical form to fit the triangular space above the entrance to the Gallery. In September 1919, however, after a bunch of niggling disputes with the trustees (all male probably), her commission was scrapped. The space that should have been filled with her approved chariot race sculpture was left blank. It's been left like that ever since. Now, close to a century later, it's up for grabs.

Let's get real. The space can't be filled with some dreary old thing drawn from ancient Western history, like a chariot race or some boring Anzac theme. No. It's got to be a contemporary image, something striking. Linked to the Australian past maybe, but in a way that resonates with the here and now. Which is where Marvic Laredo fits in. The Paraguayan settlement pointed to a new and better society, as at Cosme, and later as dreamed by Che Guevara. A win by an avant garde *female artist with a big theme of that kind would be just what's needed. It would also show how unfair the former trustees were to penalise Dohra Ohlfsen, simply because she was a woman.*

Think about it. The present bunch of trustees might even finish up being forced to apologise for what was done by their predecessors. So no more preaching, please. If you have any feeling for what the world needs right now, in a post-modern age, then please persist with your enquiries. Let me have something I can use as soon as possible. Along the way you might even find time to read the poem I've written.

And there it was. At the foot of Anita's email, the poem. As if it said all that had to be said. He had scanned it dutifully, then again, and more thoughtfully. He realised as he read it, within a deeper recess of his being, that the writing of such a poem, and the memories it conjured up, meant everything to her. It was called: *At My Mother's Desk.*

*Her typewriter in its usual
place, its keyboard stilled,
but stilled as if all set
to clatter as she wished.
It will go to an attic now,
but even in that other world
it will be as it always was,
the muse she wrestled with,
striving daily to extract
some meaning from its store
until the right word came:
a prize to end the struggle,
promising so much more.*

*Tempted by times past
to tap out some final word
to bring her back to me,
I search for what to say,
but nothing seems to come,
save for the memory of her
at her desk, the daily task,
the keys all set to clatter.*

Somewhere in the silence,
no matter where, or how,
I will soon find what I need,
fighting for the right word,
and here, beside her, now.

9

THE MAESTRO'S VISIT

The string of coloured lights above the performance area had been switched off, bringing about a quiet transformation of the scene before him. The musicians had reached the end of their bracket and were about to step down from their little bandstand. The couples abandoned the dance floor. They exchanged smiles and back-chat, gossiping as they drifted back to their tables.

Waiters kept moving purposefully to and fro, attending to the needs of their customers. Their mood, now that the music had come to an end, was polite, but seemed less cheerful than when the stage was illuminated by the coloured baubles.

'How quickly the present becomes the past,' the Maestro observed, watching the players leave the stage, one by one. 'And how much we lose when it does. The memory of their instruments and the music they made to lift our spirits is wonderful – but less than the melodies we heard as they played. Unless, of course, we reconstruct their performance and turn it into something else. A story or imagined performance of a different kind. An entirely new experience. Enchanting in its own way.'

Ian knew from the many hours he had spent with the Maestro over the years, pondering questions presented to them by colleagues in the course of their work, or by the shards and artefacts they had unearthed, that his companion was simply thinking aloud, and his thoughts weren't necessarily confined to the matter at hand, the departure of the musicians. What the Maestro said aloud was often just a fragment of a larger picture, only a faint reflection of the thoughts taking shape in his mind about the meaning of the scene before him.

While listening to the music they had reviewed the lack of reliable information about Marvic Laredo, and the nature of Ian's email exchanges with his increasingly restive sister. The time had come, the Maestro had agreed, just before the musicians lowered their instruments, to tell Anita plainly that her project in its present form was ill-advised. It wouldn't work. She had to reconfigure her proposed entry for the competition by coming up with an image based upon a clearer and more engaging story. Something closer to home, drawn not from some discordant clamour in times past but from the flow of her personal experience.

'A visual requiem for her mother perhaps.' The Maestro's ruminations about the future of Anita's project, it seemed, were still affected by a distillation of the music that had been floating past them as they talked. 'A composition of some sort, as in her poem. But reaching out to an audience beyond her.'

Ian could tell from the speaker's thoughtful tone that no answer was expected to these possibilities, so he let the silence between them settle. He shared his companion's view that Anita had to be talked out of her current plan. Unfortunately, however, the alternatives that had just been canvassed didn't seem enough. Ideas of that kind, like Ian's error in mentioning his father's attachment to the 'Mosman stone' were risky. The passionate tone of Anita's responsive email, and the poem it contained, showed that any further suggestions about what could be done to improve her prospects of winning the competition were bound to be greeted with suspicion. It was clear from other recent emails that she and her friend Kim Guest felt sure their findings confirmed the importance of her project. They were determined to keep going.

These findings, Anita had explained, reinforced by another communication from the museum curator in Havana, established that Pombo and other survivors of Che's campaign had certainly spent a few nights in Sydney on their way back to Cuba. One of them was a Bolivian journalist who was reputed to have fought in the Chaco war and, in later years, had written some pieces about Che and his relationship with Fidel Castro. These included an article published by the Liberation News Service in the early 1970s about Castro's various confrontations with the United States in the Nixon era.

Of equal importance, the emails indicated, was Anita's realisation, that a passage in her mother's manuscript about her time in the LNS newsroom described a reporter resembling the Bolivian journalist. He knew so much about Che's personal life and the customs of the Guarani people in the Chaco region. Anita was particularly intrigued by a line on the same page suggesting that Lucy Thornton may have met the man in Sydney as part of the group returning to Cuba: *I remembered him, speaking of Che, as one who would live beneath the bridge, forever.*

There was much else in this chapter of the autobiography about Lucy's time on the Columbia campus and her work with the LNS team, but it was only now, Anita said, in the light of their further research, that she had managed to read between the lines and grasp her mother's true meaning.

So now she relied on Ian to press ahead with his enquiries. If the inferences based on Anita's further research could be substantiated by a meeting with Canela Dochera, or even Laredo himself, these would strengthen her entry. It would show that the visionary depicted in her work of art – Che's Paraguayan-born comrade, Marvic Laredo – had links not only to Australian history but to Anita's mother, and thus to Anita herself, the artist behind the entry. This was bound to be of interest to the trustees in their role as judges of the competition.

Her recent emails weren't the only ones in which Anita's friend from the art collective, Kim Guest, had made an appearance. This simply heightened Ian's feeling of apprehension. He could recall an earlier exchange of emails in which, puzzled by a letter signed 'K.Guest', he had enquired of Anita, in a tone that he now saw was probably too jocular, whether the said Guest he had noticed in passing was a man or a woman. His question had evoked an immediate and somewhat condescending (or pitying) reply. A question like that in contemporary times, he was told, was old-fashioned at best, misogynistic and therefore utterly laughable at worst. *Kim was Kim. Kim was a person.* In these more enlightened times (both words were underlined) that was all Ian was entitled to know.

Now that the silence between them had lengthened, Ian turned back to the Maestro, and began running through the matters troubling him. He completed his overview by returning to what was weighing most heavily upon him. Could he be sure that Anita's hunt for information about Laredo was ill-advised? If so, in the light of her recent reply, reinforced by the deeply-felt poem about her mother, could she actually be persuaded to let the matter drop? To look elsewhere for inspiration?

The Maestro, his plump body seated firmly at one of the Varino's elegant marble-topped tables, studied the glass of wine before him, doing his best to ignore the waiters moving about in the vicinity of the service area. He seemed refreshed by the music he had heard and the moment of silence they had just enjoyed.

He pondered the question put to him in his usual thoughtful but essentially forensic way. He began by noting that Anita's project was haunted by Laredo's ghostly presence. But Laredo was a figure with an elusive past. No birth certificate. No mention in diaries kept by others in the course of Che's final campaign. No living person encountered so far who could definitely verify his existence in human form. Carlos Qurigo's boyhood recollections of running messages in La Paz for a man who resembled Che Guevara were inconclusive. The Maestro himself couldn't recall any encounters at Café Tortoni in Buenos Aires with a journalist from Paraguay named Marvic Laredo, or ever meeting such a man in Bolivia, although he could faintly recall some articles written by a survivor of the final campaign when Che was reburied in Cuba.

All this was very puzzling, and possibly sinister. The references to Laredo in newspapers and other writings, as far back as the *el Australiano* boy soldier tag in pieces concerning the Chaco war, were certainly graphic, but they didn't necessarily establish a link to the journalist who was said to have surfaced as a member of the literary set frequenting Café Tortoni, or later as one of Che's recruits at the training camp in Cuba. Laredo's article about being appointed to spread misinformation in La Paz, his unpublished draft about the shortcomings of the campaign, his finishing up with Che at the La Higuera battle, then being present when photographs of the deceased leader were taken at Vallegrande: these could have been fabricated by a third party with an axe to grind.

'These considerations,' the Maestro mused, stroking his chin as he reviewed what they had been discussing, 'are arguably confirmed by the pencilled note added to Laredo's manuscript. It suggests that this section of his article was viewed with suspicion by some unknown person or, for one reason or another, seen as unworthy of publication. It was then treated accordingly. Never published. Which prompts me to observe in passing that although the term 'person' may be a badge of honour in your sister's circle of friends, it leaves an impression of disguise to someone of my scholastic background.' He chuckled briefly, amused by his own thought. 'A pencilled note by a figure in disguise. A masked figure perhaps! Another spectral presence in the mix.'

He must have noticed that Ian wasn't smiling. 'It follows from an overview of your enquiries to this point,' the Maestro added, in a more serious tone, 'that I give little weight to the so-called recent discoveries of your sister and the 'person' Kim Guest. The passage in your mother's unfinished autobiography about transient events in Sydney and a few years later with the LNS in New York are too vague to be taken seriously. They simply add to the shadowy cloud hovering over this entire project.'

He turned to face Ian. 'You can't attach any significance to Lucy Thornton's casual reference to *one who would live forever*. Of course Che lives. He has been alive and increasingly well-known since the day he died! His immortality has been brought about by human, not divine intervention, nourished constantly by silk-screening, pop art, graphic design, T-shirts, software, and placards raised by marketeers and protesters throughout the world. It's all here in La Paz, as we speak. All contributing to Che's after-life. And let me remind you of this. When Lucy Thornton, in the same passage of her manuscript, refers to speaking of Che *beneath the bridge,* that's open to several interpretations. There are bridges in Manhattan, not just Sydney. So let's be sensible. These so-called recent discoveries are of no assistance.'

The Maestro reached for his wine glass and took a sip. 'To all of this,' he added, on the brink of rounding off his analysis, 'let us, carefully and rationally, examine the American scholar's account of what he claims to have seen at Canela Dochera's home. An elderly man in a wheelchair. A door slammed shut to keep him out of sight. Or, putting it another way, to remove him from an uninvited caller's gaze. This is the evidence which led to Brady and Facundas forming an opinion that this third person in the house is Marvic Laredo. But this is mostly surmise – something not confirmed by Ingrid Kahn and strongly doubted by Carlos Quirigo. He described the man as simply an occasional visitor.'

'It's true,' the Maestro conceded, 'that I have used Quirigo from time to time for odd jobs of one kind or another, and have even been inclined to describe him as my 'agent' in La Paz, but that doesn't necessarily mean that I treat what he says uncritically or ignore his limitations. I'm aware, of course, that for many years he has been fascinated by the life and times of Butch Cassidy and the Sundance Kid. Were they actually involved in a payroll heist and subsequent shoot-out at San Vincente? The facts of that matter, such as they are, have never been agreed or settled. They're based on what was said initially in a blood-soaked account of the shoot-out in the April 1930 edition of *Elks,* published several decades after the event. The facts are open to question. They're malleable. From which it follows that my 'agent' can be forgiven if the version of the story he favours is eventually proved wrong. But when it comes to identifying a man in a wheelchair as a former driver in his father's 'fleet', one has to give weight to what he says. He knows the back streets of his own city, and where people sleep at night.'

'So there you have it,' the Maestro concluded. 'The creation of posters may not be far removed from the creation of imposters. Fact and fiction merge. Butch Cassidy and the Kid arrive and soon every bandit in the hinterland is claiming to be one of them. They finish eventually as movie stars on a flimsy poster. President Nixon finishes up in a Dr Strangelove cartoon. Then, a short time later, at the height of the Watergate cover-up, he's devoured by a monster lurking in a basement of the White House: the tape-recording system that had been listening to everything he said and was armed with the incriminating truth.' He paused. 'One scarcely knows what to believe. In a modern world of constant fabrication, where it is increasingly difficult to keep a grip on reality, and where truth can be fatal, the most accomplished liars may eventually rule. But in the back streets of a city, where people see and listen for themselves, they generally know more exactly what's what.'

The Maestro, who had returned to stroking his chin as he made these remarks, fixed Ian with a steady gaze. 'Some of my remarks have been made facetiously, for the sake of an enjoyable discussion. But you will have gathered by now, from everything I've said, that in my opinion you simply do not have enough to provide a convincing picture of the man in question. Laredo remains a mystery. You are therefore duty-bound to advise your sister accordingly and to urge her to let the matter drop. She has seized upon the verifiable fact that an Australian community with a radical agenda was set up in Paraguay. That was to be the source of her inspiration. But her attempt to cast it in a more contemporary form is based upon Marvic Laredo. He, for some reason as yet unknown to us, seems little more than a spectre inspired by the work of others. If that can be demonstrated, her prospects of success will come to nothing. There will only be controversy, a degree of ridicule perhaps. So she has to be warned before it is too late.'

'I've told her that already,' Ian exclaimed. 'To repeat what you've just said may not be enough. These friends of hers. This art collective. She may well be prepared to run the risk of controversy, a possibility that the story she relies on can't be proved. In the art world, these days, or so it seems, people aren't bothered by a lack of proof of this or that. Or whether a work is done with skill. What they want is novelty. They want to be excited by what's weird. In the post-modern age, critics and commentators may well be enchanted by what's ephemeral. That what they thought was true is actually false. A mere phantom.'

The Maestro placed the tips of his fingers together to form a steeple, as he often did when another thought was taking shape. 'What you say is probably correct. That is the world we live in now. But none of these people, including the artist herself, will be overly excited if it turns out that her central figure, Marvic Laredo, is indeed a real person, but with a role in the story behind your sister's work of art that is potentially offensive.'

'I'm not sure what you mean?'

'Let us assume, putting our various doubts to one side for a moment, that Laredo is actually the freedom fighter who was with Che to the very end, as portrayed in his article. That after his escape to Santiago and Sydney, he returned to Cuba and eventually went back to working as a journalist in Buenos Aires. But he did so discreetly, so as not to sully Che's reputation or embarrass his former comrades. This continued until he was called upon in the 1990s, for Che's reburial in Cuba, to provide an account of the Bolivian campaign. Let us even suppose, as suggested by a recent discovery, that one of the assignments Laredo undertook in the post-campaign period, his years of discretion, was a visit to Manhattan in the Nixon era. To write a piece about anti-Nixon speeches made by Che and Castro in earlier days. At the UN and other places.'

'I follow what you say. But where's it leading?'

'At a first glance, the events I've just described seem worth repeating. Laredo is cast in a favourable light.'

'Indeed.'

'But what else do we know, from Laredo's own account of what took place, and from what has been conveyed to you by others? What do we know about his friends?'

'I have little doubt that you know far more about his friends than I. And now that my enquiries seem to have stalled, I trust you'll be willing to share whatever else you know?'

'I saw no need to do so, originally. My hope was that while in La Paz you would find your way to the lady and her niece. That you would learn from them what you needed to know.'

'That hasn't happened. And it now seems quite unlikely that it will. I'm left groping in the dark.'

'The words you need to fill that shadowy space will have to come from me, as a means of keeping your sister on the right track. She and her friends in the art collective will be deeply distressed, and left with nowhere to go, if it turns out that Marvic Laredo had many unpleasant flaws.'

'I'm here in La Paz,' Ian felt obliged to remind him, 'to find out everything I can about Laredo and those around him. So I trust you'll take the plunge and tell me everything I need to know.'

10

AN ACTOR'S MASK

The Maestro signalled to a waiter and it wasn't long before he was on his way towards them with two glasses of wine on his tray. He positioned these neatly on their table and moved on to take some orders on the far side of the courtyard.

The Maestro took a sip of wine, as if to clear his throat or possibly to allow himself a moment in which to gather his thoughts before proceeding.

'To provide an overview of a man's flaws,' he began, 'is never easy, and especially in circumstances where not much is known about the fellow in question. I will do the best I can, although much of what I know comes from Canela Dochera, and to a certain extent from Laredo's own article. There is also a degree of speculation in what I have to say.'

He took another sip of wine. 'One scarcely knows where to begin, but a start has to be made somewhere. It emerges from his article that Marvic Laredo was close to Canela Dochera, a friend and compatriot from Paraguay. Her writing skills, as were Laredo's, were refined at Café Tortoni in Buenos Aires, a favourite haunt of Jorge Luis Borges and others. The birthplace of magic realism some now say, and other forms of speculative fiction – the art of spinning something out of nothing.

Unlike most working journalists, who aspire to write stories based on fact, here were a pair of journalists adding arrows to their quiver by consorting with masters of illusion.'

He pushed his chair away from the table as if to find a more comfortable position while settling into his tale. 'I have been to Café Tortoni myself many times. I've overheard those ingenious wordsmiths conjuring up their irresistible flights of fancy. I have little doubt that Che Guevara, in his student years in Buenos Aires, also visited that place of dreams and admired those skills. He was seeking to use skills of that kind, no doubt, when he persuaded Laredo and Canela to go to La Paz. To invent tall stories that would weaken the government and prepare the way for insurrection, in the rural areas initially, the cities in due course. But Canela wasn't just a writer. She was a member of the Kahn family and of the German colony in Paraguay established in the aftermath of the Franco-German war.'

'So many kinds of communities set up in South America,' said Ian.

'Indeed. But let me tell you a little more about the antecedents of this one. It was founded in Paraguay towards the end of the 19th century by Elizabeth Nietzsche. She and her husband set up a community called Nueva Germania on the upper reaches of the Rio Paraguay as a home for Aryan pioneers and the rebirth of German culture. Time went by and the fortunes of the colony gradually declined. Elizabeth was eventually obliged to return to Germany to care for her ailing brother, Friedrich Nietzsche, the controversial philosopher. She played a leading role after his death in drawing attention to *Thus Spoke Zarathustra* and his other books. In the 1920s she established the Nietzsche Archives near Weimar and within a few years this was supported by the Nazi Party, for the central thesis reflected in the philosopher's works, notably *The Will to Power*, was attractive to Hitler and his cohorts.

'Not surprisingly, the Nietzsche Archives and the credo of the colony established by its founder were kept in mind. Soon after Hitler came to power, Heinrich Himmler set up the Ahnenerbe Institute with a view to fostering archaeological and other forms of research that would document and eventually prove the primacy of the Aryan race. Curators at the Institute became adept at manipulating archaeological evidence as they began conjuring up images of an ancient world dominated by Aryan regimes.

'German archaeologists travelled to Cuzco and La Paz. They photographed streetscapes and sacred stones at Machu Picchu. They sketched floor plans and inscriptions at the Tiwanaku ruins near Lake Titicaca. They unearthed a sculpted head from the remnants of the ancient city, the physiognomy of which was said to reveal Nordic origins. Certain artefacts and architectural styles were said to be the creation of Nordic adventurers who reached the Andean highlands, the precursors of a special predestined civilisation. By late 1939 planning was nearly complete for a new and very substantial expedition to the Bolivian Andes. There is much to suggest that members of the Nueva Germania colony, including Canela's parents and other members of the Kahn family, were drawn into these preparations with a view to gathering persuasive evidence of an ancient master race in the Americas.

'As it happened, however, the onset and demands of World War II brought these preparations to an end. But in the post-war era various German archaeologists renewed their interest in the Andes. They did so on this occasion – or so it was said – in the pursuit of strictly scientific objectives. Canela's position has always been, as reflected in her articles and columns, that she was appalled by the earlier, utterly fanciful theories concerning Andean sites. She would have nothing to do with them. She has even pointed to her youthful marriage into the Dochera family of Spanish descent, and her later move to Buenos Aires when she left the marriage, as evidence of her disenchantment with the 1930s outlook. Nonetheless, there can be little doubt that from an early age she was mixing with Germanic opportunists, skilled in the art of manipulating data to suit the case that had to be made. They shaped their supposedly professional reports accordingly.'

The Maestro spread his hands. 'Did she cut herself loose from her antecedents? There's a question that remains to be answered. It might strike some observers of the current scene that she is accustomed to wearing a mask, and always has been. But no matter. As we know from Greek tragedies, when actors are given a mask they are freed to tell the truth. Canela could see the writing on the wall. Che was receiving insufficient support from Castro and from the Bolivian Communist Party, for both were captives to Moscow's policy of securing gains by negotiation, not by force. It seems she lost faith in Che's plan for widespread revolution throughout South America once it became clear that his insurrection in southern Bolivia was bound to fail.'

'What do you mean by 'lost faith'? Ian asked. 'Is it thought she worked against or tried to subvert Che's campaign?'

'You'll have noticed in what is described as Laredo's 'unpublished draft' that, after Che's campaign got underway, the CIA set up a special Green Beret unit outside Santa Cruz. There have been suggestions that Canela, as she began adjusting her thinking to the possibility of things going wrong, was in communication with this CIA unit. Her friends might say that she was simply trying to assess its strength to use the information for Che's benefit. Others are not so sure.

'Which brings me to another feature of Laredo's draft. We're told by the author that, towards the end of the campaign, when Laredo laid aside his original task of creating misinformation in La Paz to bring recruits to Che at the battlefront, he did so via Santa Cruz. He had time enough to liaise with the CIA Green Beret unit, before joining Che at Samaipata. If asked about a visit to the CIA base, he probably told his comrades that he was gathering information for use against the Americans. A careful reading of the unpublished draft makes it very surprising that Laredo was able to escape so easily from Vallegrande after

Che was executed. There are so many holes and unsubstantiated claims in the draft that one can begin see why a decision may have been taken that it should not be published. Hence the pencilled note to that effect. Because it gives away too much.'

'So where do all these observations lead?'

'They lead back to the question you raised initially. It may be hard to persuade your sister to let the project drop, simply because a clear account of Laredo's life and times is difficult to obtain. Does he really exist? It follows, however, from everything I have just said, that the end result of her persistence may be to venerate a supposedly heroic figure who was not only a fraudulent imposter but was possibly dancing to the tune of a female puppet-master, a woman who may have been in thrall to Nazi ideology, because of her family background, and at a later stage may have aligned herself to the strategies of the CIA.'

Ian took a deep breath as he tried to make sense of this. 'A double agent of sorts,' he murmured.

The Maestro placed a hand on his sleeve, gently, as if to console him. 'I may have said too much – or too much all at once. The complexity of human lives. The mystery of the inner self. So much to fathom. We judge others by their actions, ourselves by our intentions, with what is written often being a mixture of the two. According to Nietzsche, there are no facts, only interpretations. In the end, everything comes down to a critique of the stories told. What are we to make of the texts where your enquiry started? Laredo's article, a memoir of sorts, was written to commemorate Che's reburial – or so we are led to believe – but was accompanied by an unpublished draft telling of chaos, failure and death.'

'Keep that in mind,' the Maestro added. 'The question of what was really being said. A memoir's claim on our attention is that it purports to be presenting certain facts that, once brought together, amount to a coherent narrative. But facts are different to truth, and truth is not the same as insight. Memoirs resemble historical narratives insofar as they purport to be based on facts, and seem to assert that what is said is true – that is, the facts and matters mentioned in the text can be verified. It's this assertion that puts them on the other side of the line to a work of fiction. But if a memoir is the work of an imposter, or is shown to be fraudulent, because the person who claims to be describing his or her experiences couldn't possibly have experienced what is described, then shock and bewilderment follows.

'It might well be that a work of fiction will sometimes tell the truth far better than a work purporting to be based on personal experience. In the writing of a memoir, facts are often excluded, or glossed over or embellished, as the author seeks to protect his or her reputation, or the reputation of a friend who might be affected by what is written. Hence it may sometimes be safer and more persuasive to remove the risk of shock and disbelief by characterising the *entire* narrative as simply a work of fiction. If it's fiction, we're untroubled by what seems far-fetched because we've been invited to think of it as make-believe. Nonetheless, the story may leave us with an instinctive sense that what has been said is indeed true.'

The Maestro smiled companionably as he often did while appraising shards uplifted from the inscrutable earth or inspecting Jesuit files at Tarija. 'It comes down to this perhaps. In an attempt to appease your sister you can press ahead with your attempt to interview Canela Dochera and find out who exactly is living in her house. There is still a possibility of achieving this because it seems from what you say that her niece Ingrid is sympathetic. She may yet be persuaded to contrive a meeting. And I'll certainly do what I can to procure such a meeting for you, if that's what you want.'

'On the other hand,' he continued, 'you can draw together all the fruits of your enquiries and present them to your sister as a work of fiction, a story in which the point is made along the way that the figure at the centre of your quest doesn't exist. Moreover, even if he did, his character is disreputable, tainted by his links to Nazis and possibly to the CIA, as a factor in Che's downfall. An image of him should therefore not be used to advance the prospects of a work of art. A story of that kind, couched as fiction, may convey a more convincing truth than simply a factual account of what happened here and there in La Paz in the course of your research, an account which is flawed by shaky inferences, areas of surmise and an inability to interview some crucial witnesses.'

Ian stared at his companion. 'Are you seriously suggesting that I get my sister to abandon what I've increasingly come to see as a misguided project by reducing the enquiries I've made on her behalf to a work of fiction? To some sort of fable from which she can learn a lesson? As if I were an actor speaking the truth from behind a mask?'

The Maestro sat back in his chair, glass in hand, a tender smile on his face, pleased apparently that he had managed to evoke such a strong reaction. 'Fiction can be a form of persuasion, You should read my article to that effect in the Berlin journal *Am Rande der Nacht. At the Edge of Night*. I called my article *Truth in Fiction*.'

'Very neat.'

The Maestro must have sensed that Ian had too much on his mind to cope with such suggestions. 'But no matter.' He placed a companionable hand on Ian's sleeve. 'You can get to things like that in due course. In the meantime, you must proceed as you wish. But we seem to be agreed on the most important thing. Your sister's project isn't viable. The central character, Laredo, even if he does or did exist, can only be described as deeply flawed. Think on it. Marvic Laredo with Che at Samaipata, after visiting the CIA. One way or another Anita has to be talked down from her ledge, before she, and those around her, come to grief.'

The Maestro pointed. 'Look! The musicians are back. Well and truly rested. We must wait and see what they play next. The play's the thing.'

11

ANITA'S EMAIL

That evening, still pondering his meeting with the Maestro, Ian sat up late in his hotel room, drafting a short but emphatic report to his sister. He laid out all the pros and cons, and the reasons why it would be most unwise to proceed as she wished.

Next morning, when he sat down to send his painfully-constructed message to her, one that was bound to cause her disappointment, even anger, he was brought to a sudden halt. There, on the computer screen, he found another lengthy email from her, as if sent to frustrate him before he could get his own message across.

Ian. A quick email to let you know that my friend Kim Guest has made an important discovery. While corresponding with the curator in Havana who has been so helpful, she sifted through a bibliography in one of the recommended books. She came across an article by two Spanish journalists, Bertrand de la Grange and Maite Rico, published some years ago in the journal Letras Libres. *They called it* Operación Che: Historia de una mentiro de Estado. *It was published 10 years ago in 2007 to coincide with the anniversary of Che's death. It says that the bones at Vallegrande identified as Che's weren't the remains of his body! The so-called 'discovery' of these remains in 1997, followed by the reburial at the commemorative site* in Cuba, was simply a performance, a stage show devised by Castro to revive the revolutionary spirit in Cuba at a time of economic downturn.

The authors of this article came up with some riveting evidence. They named witnesses who were known to have taken possession of some of Che's personal belongings – the same things that were said to have been found in the recently-discovered grave at Vallegrande. The bones allegedly 'proving' identification were discovered with others in a common grave. The authors reminded readers of what was said about the original burial: Che was buried alone. Then what about the unexplained failure of the Cuban government to conduct a DNA test? This was promised after the so-called Che remains were found, but never done.

The Cuban government did its best to discredit the authors. Castro's cronies rambled on about supposedly scientific opinions at the time of the reburial. But many people don't believe them.

All this, of course, bears upon you're enquiries on my behalf. If doubts remain about the identity of the person buried at Vallegrande after the final battle, and if the reburial in Cuba 30 years later was mainly a stage show, a piece of propaganda, then this might explain Marvic Laredo's unpublished article. Marked 'unpublished draft' because it revealed too much.

So Che may have survived the final battle. Laredo's draft doesn't give details of exactly when and where his life ended. Initially, he was said to have died of his wounds up at La Higuera, but this was retracted, and then he was supposedly executed when orders came in from somewhere or other. Which brings us back to the question Fidel Castro posed in the speech he made at the reburial of Che's remains in Cuba: what was a man from the US government doing up there when Che was wounded and taken prisoner? The CIA is capable of anything, including the creation of fake death-bed photographs. There was obviously a squabble going on between the American and the Bolivian authorities as to whether Che should be finished off immediately or kept alive for interrogation and eventually brought to trial. Observers at that time may well have been led astray by a *skilful cover-up like Nixon's Watergate a few years later.*

Laredo is the key to all this. And this leads us to another crucial question. Did Laredo have any descendants? There are passages in the 'unpublished draft' which point in that direction. He suggests that he lived quietly after returning to Cuba, but we now know from my mother's manuscript that he was in New York at a wild time in the Nixon era. It seems from his 'draft' that upon returning to Buenos Aires, and eventually to La Paz he 'settled down' (to use his words). So you can see how important your enquiries are.

If you can't find Laredo, then look for his descendants. One way or another, you have to achieve a meeting with Canela Dochera. Talking to her will fill in a whole lot of blank spaces.

Please let me hear from you as soon as possible. But when you write to me, please take care what you say. I've found in reading one of your emails out loud to our group that you often risk causing offence. You may see your work on foreign sites as an attempt to understand and learn from another culture, but to many decent people of goodwill, archaeologists are involved essentially in acts of cultural misappropriation. My entry in the competition is one of many steps towards trying to end atrocities like that. The winning entry and the image above the entrance to the Gallery must have nothing to do with old-fashioned stereotypes drawn from a purely Western tradition. We have to look further afield. Which is why links to South America via Laredo, or even to some of his descendants, are so important. They will point the way to a different sort of historical record. Something entirely new. Dreams of a better world. So please don't let me down. Anita.

Ian closed the message on the screen. Abruptly. He folded his arms, staring at a faint reflection of himself in the vacant patch of glass. He took a few deep breaths, slowly and conscientiously, aware that he had come close to hammering out a furious reply. He wanted to say that he was sick and tired of her pleas for pushing ever-further with his enquiries, and more than weary of the assistance of Kim Guest and others in her group.

He had to admit, however, after a moment, that there was a certain force in what she had said. In these changing times, there were many others who thought as she did – including judges of prizes who favoured works by artists and writers with innovative views and irreproachable antecedents. It wasn't so long ago, he seemed to recall, that an Australian writer had won a major literary prize for a work about the Holocaust by posing as the descendant of a Ukrainian victim of the era. There had been other equally astonishing cases of authors winning approval by creating what seemed to be a fashionable identity.

All this meant that he would have to rewrite the email he had prepared. That was clear. It struck him also, having regard to what she had said, that it would probably be best, before he sent his message to her, to find out whether the Maestro had been able to secure a meeting with Canela Dochera. So much now depended on what the lady knew and what she might be willing to say.

Her account might be the only way of bringing all the wild speculation to an end. It was open to a cabaret artist perhaps, or to a satirist from Café Tortoni, to cast light on folly by staging an outlandish skit. This could dramatize the loss of common sense that made bizarre depictions of reality seem almost plausible. But it was not, of course, the way an archaeologist like himself usually worked. So far, the power shaping the course of his investigation had been exercised by strident voices in Anita's group. The time had come to speak in some more convincing way to this form of power. It had to be done, and done decisively.

12

SOME OTHER WORLD

The pace of his trip to La Paz was quickening. Cryptic messages were coming at Ian from all sides. In random bursts. Like transmissions from outer space. As if construing the gaps and pauses, reading between the lines, was the only way to work out what had to be done.

At the hotel reception desk he was handed a message from the Maestro. His colleague must have found a moment between meetings with the UN delegation to pull some strings. Or had Ingrid talked her aunt into meeting the Australian visitor? The message named a time for Ian to meet Carlos Quirigo at the Blue Note. He would then be told where he was to see Canela Dochera. He would be given directions.

Back in his room, before setting off, Ian found a new email message from Anita. It underlined what she had said a few hours earlier. It added to his anxiety and brought with it a mounting sense of bewilderment.

After working right through the available documents, Anita explained – Laredo's writings, her mother's manuscript, some further research – she and Kim Guest had joined the dots. They were now convinced that Lucy Thornton, having met and flirted with Laredo on his fleeting visit to Sydney, had almost certainly entered into a fully-fledged romance with the freedom fighter some years later. During

Lucy's time with the Liberation News Service in New York.

They were still checking the relevant dates – but *Lucy and Marvic Laredo could have had a child together!* Anita would let him know what came out of her further research, but all of this was certainly *thrilling*. It lent an extra layer of meaning to the project. In the meantime, it was more important than ever that Ian keep at it. Complete his enquiries in La Paz. Find out what's what.

A passionate liaison. Checking dates. Not just a lover, perhaps a long-lost father emerging from the mist. What next? Ian set off for the Blue Note with a heavy heart. Far from abandoning her project, Anita seemed to be plunging in ever-deeper. *Thrilling* for her perhaps, but not so for others, and especially not for her brother. Surely, not now, at this late stage, Anita, out there in the dark, banging the missing father drum! Yet he knew he had to find out more about Laredo, from Canela Dochera, or from anyone who knew. Not for the reasons Anita had in mind. Clarity was required for the sake of his sanity and for the sanity of those around him.

Upon reaching the Blue Note, he found Carlos was at the bar and into his second beer. He was primed to give directions to Canela's home. But this was accompanied, inevitably, by Carlos-style chit-chat and some vaguely ominous observations about the place in question.

Canela's home, according to Carlos, had been constructed by a German building firm in the 1920s to serve as an inn for travellers from afar: Europe, England and the United States. It closed down after World War II and had passed through several hands since then. The dining room had been divided into living quarters, but the library overlooking the street, used as a lounge for guests back in the day, was still intact.

The former inn's features, Carlos went on to say, included not only a staircase in the front hall but a small lift in an alcove to one side of the flight of stairs. He shivered as he said it and gave a solemn warning: *Don't use that lift!* His warning was accompanied by another movement of the shoulders, a kind of shudder, like a dog shaking off water. 'It's smaller than a miner's cage, that lift. Metal bars and grilles. And a flickering yellow light overhead that often fails. Like the power to the lift itself.'

He felt obliged to explain. 'Once I was trapped in that lift for several hours, with only a cockroach on the mat for company. Nothing to look at but dead flies in the overhead light shield. Never again, I said to myself. Use the staircase if you have to, although no one is usually allowed upstairs. Do you know how they got me out, trapped between the kitchen in the basement and the ground floor? I kept calling out, until I heard a shout from below. So I did what I was told. Lifted the mat on the floor. Raised the trapdoor beneath it. Nothing there but a deep black hole. Until I saw the old guy's torch come on. Way down in the shaft, and to one side. He was telling me how to climb down, holding on to the cable and using some niches in the wall.'

Carlos made a wincing, whistling sound as he relived the unpleasant experience. 'A cable covered with grease.' He opened his hands as if to exhibit the filth that the palms of his hands had been forced to grasp. 'Grease and slime everywhere. And just a couple of toeholds in the wall. And way down there, a heap of rubbish at the bottom of the shaft. Bones of former guests for all I knew.' He paused for effect. 'So stay away from that lift.'

He then handed Ian a slip of paper. 'Follow the arrows on the map. And knock loudly when you get there, because no one ever seems to hear anything in that place.'

Jovial again, he slapped Ian on the back in what was obviously meant to be a comradely gesture. 'Good-bye and good luck.'

At the first intersection on the map Ian came to a bus shelter with a bunch of would-be passengers besieging a dusty coach that had just pulled in. Mostly Aymaran women in bowler hats and voluminous skirts, burdened with woven shopping bags. One woman was holding a wire cage with a bird inside it. A silhouette with folded wings. Ian waited while the women pushed and shoved each other onto the bus. When the path was clear, he edged forward, map in hand. It was hard to read the names of the streets scrawled on the scrap of paper.

He rounded a corner and found himself in an old cobblestone street, sloping upwards. Picturesque, save for a vacant yard close to the corner. Within the yard, a line of stunted trees along a brick wall led to a cluster of vines and a flowering bougainvillea overhanging a tin shack, some cars for sale nearby. An old hoarding on wooden stilts stood by the gate, facing the street. It was blank, just a tattered white screen. A man in paint-spattered overalls, brush in hand, was standing beside a large step ladder. About to start work, apparently, attaching some new posters to the screen, or roughing out some images to fill the blank space confronting him. He was surrounded by a half-circle of buckets and some cans of paint.

On the opposite side of the street the building frontages were pushed right up to the sidewalk. Some of the houses had small second-floor balconies, with room enough for flower boxes below the shuttered windows. A couple of houses had flowering vines on their balconies and one even had a potted palm tree behind the handrail. Close by Ian could see a more impressive structure. He set off in that direction, for this was Canela's home according to the cross on his map. He ascended a short flight of steps to reach the front door. It was painted black and on a small name-plate he could read the name *Cochera*. Beneath the plate was a brass knocker resembling a fist holding two crossed hammers.

Somewhere down the street a voice was shouting. When he looked around he saw a man on the sidewalk staring upwards, a hand cupped to his mouth. Above, a figure on a balcony seemed to be shifting furniture, using a rope to lower a chair to the man on the path below. It hit the ground and toppled sideways, before the helper could save it.

Ian turned back to the door and knocked briskly. When the silence lengthened, he knocked again, but louder, putting the symbolic hammers to practical use. He was expecting the door to be opened by Ingrid, for Canela's niece must have been told that he would call at this hour. But it turned out that he was to be invited in by a maid, a demure young lady with long black plaits, carrying a tiny bell. This she tinkled, while edging away from him, inwards, but still keeping an eye on him. When she sounded her little bell again Ian could hear another, fainter bell somewhere deep within the house, as if a warning had been given.

The simplicity of the front steps was now displaced by a glimpse of the elegant interior, a space that once must have once served as a foyer to the former inn. He had reached what seemed to be a large, high-ceilinged hall with a central staircase leading to an upper floor. The red carpet on the stairs was fixed to each step with brass bars. There were alcoves on each side. In one of these Ian could see what appeared to be the metal grid door of the elevator Carlos had spoken of. Set into the walls beside each of the alcoves were recesses occupied by ornate vases. He could also see a corridor leading to the back of the house, and there were a number of rooms adjoining the hall.

As he looked around, Ian felt as if he had gone back many years in time, to the between-wars era perhaps. Heavy curtains by the front windows were draped, with folds held by tie-backs of thick braided silk. There was a faded carpet on the floor. On armchairs by one of the front windows he could see doilies and squares of embroidery. A long sofa upholstered with dark green velvet stood against a side wall with a huge gilt-framed painting above it, a picture of the famous 'tin mountain' at Potosi.

He could hear a TV set blaring somewhere nearby. The sound pricked his memory. If he chose to track down the TV set, would he have the same experience as the American scholar, chancing upon an elderly fellow in a wheelchair? He quickly decided that this wasn't a risk worth running, so he turned back to the maid to let her know why he had come, handing her a note to be taken to her mistress.

She nodded, dark eyes still upon him, then led the way to the nearest door. With a simple gesture, she invited him to enter. He found himself in what looked like a sizable library. Books lined the wooden shelves from floor to ceiling. In a corner of the room a tall wooden ladder had been placed in a convenient position to provide access to the upper shelves.

Two tinted windows, flanked by curtain drapes, overlooked the street. A desk with a reading light on it was situated at the far end of the room, attended by two old-fashioned leather armchairs on a Persian carpet. Paintings and etchings had been hung in spaces between the book shelves. In addition to landscapes, the works on display included Piranesi prints and reproductions from Goya's *Los caprichos* series. One of these, *The Sleep of Reason,* with its image of a sleeping man slumped over his desk, haunted by a flock of owls with outspread wings, was positioned above a black lacquer cabinet. A silver platter on the box displayed an array of wine glasses.

Nearby, close to the centre of the spacious room, stood a round table occupied by newspapers and magazines, with enough space left for a cluster of oriental carvings and other curios. These included a bejewelled paper-knife and a finely-carved conch shell showing two classical lovers clinging to one another in a fond embrace.

The maid quietly withdrew. As he used to do in his father's library, Ian strolled across to the nearest shelf, curious to know what he might find. A small inscription attached to the shelf said: *Books for Guests.* A remnant of former days, presumably, when the premises had served as an inn. On this shelf he noticed a row of classic texts, including novels by Cervantes, Tolstoy, Balzac, Dickens and Conrad. On the next shelf stood Robert Louis Stevenson's *Dr Jekyll and Mr Hyde* and Conan Doyle's *Sherlock Holmes.* There was also a handsomely-bound volume containing the two famous works by Lewis Carroll: *Alice's Adventures in Wonderland* and *Alice Through the Looking-Glass.* He plucked this from the shelf and turned to the first page, pleased to find a familiar passage.

When the Rabbit took a watch out of its waistcoat, and looked at it, and then hurried on, Alice started to her feet, for it flashed across her mind that she had never before seen a rabbit with either a waistcoat pocket, or a watch to take out of it, and burning with curiosity, she ran across the field after it, and was just in time to see it pop down a large rabbit-hole under the hedge. In another moment down went Alice after it, never once considering how in the world she was going to get out again.

Some skilfully-conceived etchings scattered throughout the book were enough to remind Ian of the heroine's various adventures below ground: her pursuit of the white rabbit, then adrift in her own tears after nibbling the mushroom that made her larger or smaller, the Mad Hatter's tea party with the March Hare and other extraordinary guests, scoldings by an irate Queen, a riddle about the raven and the writing desk …

He closed the book, and was about to put it back, when he realised that he was being observed. An elderly woman had entered the library and was standing by the door. She was neat and straight, with grey hair, carefully waved; she was clearly of German descent. She had high cheekbones and wrinkles at the corners of her striking blue-grey eyes. His feeling that she must have been a beauty in her day quickly subsided as she approached, for the cool inquisitorial look she gave him could not be disregarded.

With her steady gaze upon him, he found he couldn't turn away to put the book back on the shelf, so he simply put it down on the round table.

The woman smiled at his momentary confusion, but without any real warmth. 'You can have that book if you wish.' She took a few more steps towards him to reach a position on the far side of the table. 'Those books!' She gestured. 'They look as though they'll stay on that shelf forever. But no one reads them any more. Are we beholding flotsam of the past or jetsam from a world to come? A time arrives when you have to get rid of such things.'

That said, she introduced herself by holding up his note. 'Canela Dochera. As you expected. And you are Ian Thornton, I am led to believe.'

Ian didn't quite know what to make of these remarks, or of her unwavering appraisal of him. It seemed best to come quickly to the reason for his visit. 'You'll know from the note that there are things I want to discuss. But I must begin by thanking you.'

'Thanking me for what?'

'For agreeing to see me.'

Her blue-grey eyes were still upon him. 'My niece Ingrid seems to think well of you. But you'll understand that my presence here establishes that there is no further need for you to talk to her.'

This quiet but forceful ultimatum didn't seem to require an answer. So he ignored it, saying only: 'It was good of her to intervene on my behalf. I trust she made it clear that I'm simply looking for some information – in a friendly way. On behalf of my sister in Sydney. She's an artist. In the course of her work she's taken an interest in the life and times of a man from Paraguay called Marvic Blas Laredo.'

'My niece Ingrid has no power to 'intervene'. Nor any power to determine how I use my time. I'm meeting you because of what I've heard from several different sources. You're working with Senor Kurt Meissner, I believe? He likes to be known as 'the Maestro'. Out of vanity, I presume.'

'If he's the one who has arranged this meeting, then I'm indebted to him. But let me assure you again that I'm here in a friendly way.'

'So you keep saying. But I'll be the judge of that. And of the purpose of this meeting.'

She reached into the folds of her skirt and produced some photographs which she handed to him. The first showed Ian standing beside Carlos Quirigo on a street corner, with a row of helmeted *polizia* in blue uniforms blocking the entrance to Plaza Murillo. They were facing a bunch of protesters with upraised placards.

This snapshot must have been taken surreptitiously, probably by the Aymaran woman selling nuts and figs with whom Carlos had effected the exchange of cell-phones. From her position, on the sidewalk below the pictured scene, a foreshortening effect in the photo suggested that Ian was standing virtually under a placard held by one of the protesters, almost as if he were a member of the group. Actually, he and Carlos had been standing on the opposite side of the street, closer to the camera.

'This gives a false impression,' he informed Canela in a level tone, not sure what she hoped to achieve by showing it to him, but not wishing to annoy her. 'I was there. But not quite like that.'

She held out her hand to retrieve the photo, her face impassive. 'For most people in our modern world, the truth of a matter is what it seems to be.'

She handed him another photo. It showed Ian sitting with Javier Facundas in the Varino courtyard. He glanced at it quickly and gave it back. In the next photo, there he was again, at a different table in the same courtyard, this time with the Maestro, the musicians on their little bandstand in the background.

He returned this too, pleased to see it was the last of the batch.

'I like to know what's happening in my corner of the old city,' Canela Dochera observed. 'You've been moving about the place, apparently, in what you like to call a friendly way. Whispering to this one and that one. So the time has come to set you straight.'

The photos were back in her skirt pocket, but her gaze was still upon him. 'My niece seems to think you can be trusted. To see things as they really are. And to keep what you see to yourself. But even if she's wrong in that, the greater risk is that unless you hear what I have to tell you, you'll give too much weight to what you've heard from others and finish up being led astray. I'm here to acquaint you with that risk, and to warn you that your enquiries could have dire consequences, for you, and for those around you. The photos I've just shown you will play a part in that, if necessary.'

Without waiting for a reply, she made a gesture and led the way to the writing desk and chairs at the far end of the room.

The desk was bare save for a small glass inkwell, an expanse of blotting paper, a few books and a tiny hand-bell beside the reading lamp. Its top was inlaid with fine hand-tooled leather marked out by a gilt geometric pattern at the borders. The same pattern was visible on the leather strips in which the pristine sheet of blotting paper was encased. Ian doubted that much use was made of this desk, but it fitted the library well, and certainly looked impressive.

'We will sit.' She slipped into one of the two leather armchairs by the desk, and waited while he settled into the other. 'So I can take you back to Paraguay,' she continued. 'Which is where the story begins.'

There had been no outward softening of her manner or tone of voice, but it seemed to Ian that it suited her, perhaps for the reasons she had just given, to make sure that he was properly informed. He needed, for the time being at least, to listen quietly, as if he were a confidant. 'I know a little about the various expatriate settlements in Paraguay,' he murmured, taking care not to break the mood by mentioning Laredo's name, 'and the Chaco war. But I'd like to know more.'

'You know from your colleague, the so-called Maestro,' she began, 'that I was born and brought up in the Nietzschean colony. But I felt obliged to move away from my parents and family members. Including my brother – Ingrid's father. I had to move because those of German descent were generally seen as linked to the pre-war Nazi ideology and to the archaeological ventures funded by Himmler's Ahnenerbe Institute. To my mind, all of that, the search for Aryan ruins and relics was a delusion. I married into the well-known Dochera family in an attempt to sever those links and make my own life – but to no avail. In the post-war era Germans in that area lived under a cloud of suspicion, irrespective of whether they were too young to have seen war service. This played a part in my decision to leave the marriage and work as a journalist in Buenos Aires. Then La Paz. With the name Dochera I could pass as a person of Spanish descent.

'In La Paz, especially, I thought of myself as someone who had grown up at last. I realised that in my earlier life when I behaved well I was doing so only because I had no good reason not to. Now I could be whoever I wanted to be, and do as I thought best, immune to Nazi ideology or the burden of Aryan myths. But inevitably it proved impossible to shake off all traces of my upbringing. After the war, my brother asked me to look after some German archaeologists. Scholars of a younger generation who had visited Paraguay and were on their way to La Paz. I had to comply. And I did so again later.

'While driving my brother's friends to Tiwanaku and other sites, it struck me that these younger men, unlike the pre-war archaeologists of my father's era, were strictly, and indeed admirably, scientific in their outlook. They were entirely rational, but at the same time passionately committed to the unravelling of mysteries that would enlarge their understanding of the world. Your colleague, the Maestro, was among them. When they talked among themselves, it was more than exciting. It was bewitching.'

She leaned forward, reaching for one of the books on the desk, which must have been placed there for a purpose. 'I can well remember the day, over a picnic lunch by the Sun Gate at Tiwanaku, when one of them read aloud a passage from Nietzche's *Ecce Homo*.'

She opened the book at a page marked with a yellow paper slip and began to read in a soft but urgent voice: *And now, therefore, having been long on the way, we Argonauts of the ideal, our courage perhaps greater than our prudence, often shipwrecked and bruised, saw before us that undiscovered country, whose frontiers no one has yet seen, a land lying beyond all other known lands and hiding places, such that our curiosity and lust for possession are brought to a pitch of extreme excitement. Nothing on earth can satisfy us.*

She returned the book to its place on the desk. 'They were principally excited by what Tiwanaku might reveal, but I was excited to have chanced upon something deeper in myself. For that is the value of literature. It can shape thoughts and awake emotions we didn't know we had. It can discover truths within us that we feel but can't see. It was at about that time that Tania came to La Paz on Che's behalf. She was a young woman also with a German background, and close to my own age. I heard in what she said about Che's plans an echo of the zeal Nietzsche had described. She recruited me to her cause, and we became the best of friends. We worked together to set up the various folklore groups that would be of use to Che in fostering a mood for change. Everything we did was done carefully, under cover.

'I was delighted when Che himself arrived. He was in disguise, of course, but I could sense his power. In the short time he was with us in La Paz he spoke so passionately about his quest for widespread revolution. Guerrilla warfare in the Bolivian countryside to begin with. Then the cities. For Tania and me, this dream seemed so promising. We embarked, as if to reach another and far better shore. When Che set off to establish the base camp at Nancahuazu our buoyant mood and sense of purpose enriched our lives for many months. But after a while, I have to admit, some of us – and I was such a one – began to harbour doubts about Che's tactics. But we kept this to ourselves.'

She leaned back in her chair. 'The guerrilla force he had assembled was very small, and with comparatively few Bolivians. They were heading to the Guarani region where the Chaco war was fought, but none of them could speak the local language. Che's book *Guerra de Guerillas* was based entirely on his experience in the Cuban revolution. It didn't fit Bolivia. Gains achieved by the mining workers at Potosi some years earlier had diluted anti-government feelings, especially in the rural areas. Our doubts about his tactics were heightened by the refusal of the local Communist Party to provide support.'

'Was Che aware of this?' Ian interjected.

'He was indeed. And Tania was well-aware of this after her visit to Che's encampment with the secretary of the Party. The Party spokesman voiced his opposition to what was afoot. He challenged Che's insistence that the insurrection be led exclusively by Che himself.'

Canela made a despairing gesture. 'While Tania was at Che's encampment, I had a meeting in La Paz with a special friend from Havana. There would be no help from there, he told me, because Moscow was opposed to Che's plans. There were also doubts in Havana about Che's capacity and his dissident beliefs. As Minister for Industry in Castro's government, Che had fallen out with most of his fellow ministers. He wanted to move straight to Utopian Communism, in which everyone was paid according to their needs, with virtuous sentiments the only incentive to work hard. His ill-fated attempt to orchestrate a revolution in the Congo was badly-planned and failed miserably. Tribalism was strong in that corner of the world and political awareness virtually non-existent. Most of the recruits there were mystified by Che's Marxist rhetoric. They turned their backs on it. Che eventually gave up, and had to sneak back to Cuba secretly, cloaked in various disguises, a way of life to which he was becoming increasingly accustomed.'

A silence fell as Canela glanced at Ian, sizing up the gringo and deciding whether it was safe to proceed. She continued: 'When Tania got back from Che's encampment, the leadership of our group felt obliged to run through all these matters with her. It was clear from her report that Che's tiny force was faltering. The local *campesinos* and Guarani people were not only withholding support, but some of them, acting as informers, were working against him. It seemed to our group that he was bound to fail, and for much the same reasons that had ended his venture in the Congo. His Bolivian dream would soon become another nightmare. It was reckless to proceed and someone had to say so. But Tania wouldn't listen. She was still enraptured. She hurried off to Che's encampment to join the remnants of his force in the field. He should have sent her straight back to La Paz. But no. He let her stay on. Until she drowned. As you know, her bullet-riddled body was found downstream.'

Canela was clearly affected by these memories. She closed her eyes for a moment. Ian waited until she was ready to resume, before putting the question he had to ask. 'Did Tania tell Che what his supporters in La Paz were thinking?'

Canela shrugged. 'No one knows the answer to that. She was killed while her friends in La Paz were still deciding what to do. News of Tania's death made things much worse. We could see that other deaths would follow, and we had no wish to see Che perish in some god-forsaken ravine. Nonetheless, soon afterwards, someone in the group must have lost their nerve or decided to try and put an end to any further bloodshed. The Bolivian high command and the CIA were provided with all we knew. The informers, whoever they were, may also have been hoping to get immunity for themselves, when the government started searching for Che's supporters. From that moment on, the rest of us had to keep our heads down and cover our tracks.'

'Including you?'

'Of course. I couldn't be sure of what I might say, if questioned. I never forgave Che for Tania's death. She was everything to me. We set forth in Che's ark as two, but our hearts and minds were fused and we soon became as one. Which was how it was meant to be – but not how it finished up. The dream we shared disappeared with her when she drowned. I was alone again, my driver my only companion. But I've always been a realist. I don't take kindly to reckless perseverance when things unravel, more lives being thrown away, even in a just cause. At first, I'd thought I could follow Che to a new world, a better place. But in the end he wasn't my hero.'

It was time for Ian to speak. 'But what about Laredo's manuscripts? They paint a picture of Che fighting bravely to the very end, with support from those behind him in La Paz. Yourself included. Names are mentioned. There's no suggestion in Laredo's writings that Che was abandoned by his friends.'

Canela smiled grimly. 'The Laredo manuscripts surfaced many years later – by which time the government in Bolivia had changed and Che had been re-invented as a martyr. The heroic legend of Che Guevara has kept growing and growing, nourished by the famous photo.'

'The Korda photo?'

Exactly. *Guerillico Heroico*. It was taken at a mass demonstration soon after the Cuban revolution brought Castro to power. During Castro's speech on that occasion, according to my friend in Havana, Che Guevara stepped into view for just a few seconds. Alberto Korda quickly snapped two frames before he disappeared from sight. The image only became widely-known after Che's death. The dark beret, the leather jacket, the resolute gaze, the unkempt good looks: these were more than enough to make Che the embodiment of radical chic. The more famous he became in death, the more widely his image has become an indestructible reality. The more that people on the left began glancing at the circumstances of his death, putting their own gloss on the main events – the hero's capture at La Higuera, the presentation of a body at the Vallegrande hospital – the more those same people began pointing accusing fingers, portraying Che as their hero, as the victim of dark betrayal. Without knowing who exactly amongst us *had* betrayed him, the members of our group had to protect ourselves by dismissing the allegations as mere rumour, by adding another gloss to the facts. They looked to me for help, the skilled magician from Paraguay and Café Tortoni.'

'What kind of help?'

'I invented a man called Marvic Blas Laredo. I cast about for bits and pieces from the lives of others to give him a plausible identity. A boy soldier in the Chaco War, like my former husband. A journalist in Buenos Aires, like me. And so on. I fabricated some notes and diaries. With the help of my special friend in Havana I prepared an article in Laredo's name for a booklet brought out to commemorate Che's reburial in Cuba. Laredo's writings, especially his 'article', confirm the heroic status of his leader and suggest that all those around him were loyal to the end. Although, if the article is read carefully, a discerning eye will notice many questions could be raised about Che's credibility and capacity.'

'As in the 'unpublished draft'?'

'Indeed. There are, of course, details within the draft concerning Che's final days that reflect what was depicted in diaries kept by others: such as Tania's fate, the confusion surrounding Che's capture, and the journey back to Cuba made later by the survivors of Che's force. The stops along the way in Santiago, Sydney and other places. But Laredo's writings are fiction. Justified by the need to cover the tracks of those instructing me who might otherwise be accused of betraying Che.'

She pointed to herself. 'These works of fiction were also a way of shoring up my own anti-authoritarian credentials. Amidst all the rumours, it was useful to suggest that Canela Dochera in particular, a Paraguayan friend of Marvic Blas Laredo, and a fellow journalist from Buenos Aires, remained loyal to Che Guevara to the very end.'

Now, at last, the lady favoured him with a faint smile, amused by this reminder of her own ingenuity, a joke at the expense of those she had been instructed to protect. 'I knew of the Australian settlement at Cosme. It wasn't far away from Elizabeth Nietzsche's German colony. There were families in that vicinity called Laredo. It occurred to me while creating my imposter that if any readers of Laredo's writings became incensed at the words and deeds attributed to *el Australiano* in his article, or dug deeper, their suspicious gaze would be focused on some interloper linked to a distant country, hard to trace and virtually invisible.'

She smiled again, but this time grimly. 'It never occurred to me, of course, that many years later some artistic opportunist from the Antipodes, would start pestering museum curators in Havana for details about Che's final days in Bolivia. The letters written by your sister were naïve, but so brimful of admiration for her idol that my special friend in Havana was worried by them. They were so effusive they almost seemed to suggest that a hero of Che's stature simply couldn't have been undone by incompetence. So he must have been a victim of foul play. Your sister's letters reminded us of the rumours we thought we had put to rest. So I told my special friend in Havana to send her the Laredo article. It took us entirely by surprise when she unexpectedly began to take an obsessive interest in the man I chose to call *el Australiano*. Nor could I foresee that these letters would lead to a loving brother – if that's what you are – appearing in La Paz, trying to find out what happened to Che and who Laredo really is.'

Ian raised a hand to stop her. 'Why are you telling me all of this? So much. Why did you agree to meet me?'

'To bring your enquiries to an end. You can tell your sister whatever you like. Whatever will satisfy her. We can't afford to have people here in South America, or in Australia – or anywhere! – raising awkward questions about Laredo or about what his writings really reveal. That is what I wish to say to you, and to you alone. You're not to repeat what I've told you. I need no promises from you. The photos I have will be enough to keep you on the straight and narrow track. The truth is what it seems to be. A gringo pictured in a protest march? Conspiring with others in the Varino courtyard? You'll have enemies on both sides of politics, and within the government, if the photos I have are passed around. The work of your team at the Chiquitos missions will be brought to a sudden halt.'

Ian spread his hands. 'Threats like that aren't needed. Your niece has obviously told you all about my enquiries, and of the doubts I have about the wisdom of my sister's project. I've been trying to persuade her to give it up, to look for inspiration closer to home. What you've said today simply underlines my intention to follow that course. I'll be discreet in what I say to her, and I'll urge her to act accordingly in what she says and does.'

'Good. We seem to have arrived at an understanding.' Canela reached for the bell beside the reading lamp, and tinkled it.

She seemed much calmer now. She raised a hand to her lips as she cleared her throat. Then she spoke in a gentler tone. 'We seem to be of one mind, which is sensible. But what next? Artists can roam in their imaginations as they please. In a peculiar way, I enjoyed creating Laredo. It took me back to the evenings I spent with Borges and his friends at Café Tortino. A detail here. Another there. A celebratory bonfire at La Higuera. A party held near Sydney Harbour Bridge for the survivors heading back to Cuba. As you write, you catch a glimpse of something. A scene. A human figure. An idea takes shape. And off you go. You work it up to its final form. Like it or not, most people's view of the past is affected by the gloss we give to it. And the same for politics, which is mostly postures and performance. The truth is what it seems to be, from doctored photos to images on TV screens and hoardings. Berets and dark eyes contributing to vast illusions. So why should I be ashamed of creating Marvic Blas Laredo. A work of art? To some extent. But for those around me at that time, a political necessity.'

'Nonetheless,' Ian interposed. 'You seem to have a feeling of ambivalence about him.'

She gave him a sharp glance. 'Of course. Art thrives on imitations of reality, sleights of hand. Politics makes use of art. But that can be dangerous. When all is said and done, political leaders and the people they serve have to keep their feet on firm ground. So do political adventurers. If they lack the competence to defend their initial gains, the vacuum will soon be filled by tyrants. Che was brave and stayed true to his beliefs. But when his dreams became unreal, he lost his way. His image is everywhere, that's true, a beacon to would-be radicals at large, especially young ones, but where does it dwell? In reality? Or in some other world? Time will tell. You can't remake the world if you don't know who you are.'

The maid had joined them now, standing quietly in the doorway. '*Es la hora de partir*,' Canela informed her. 'Our guest is leaving.'

On their way past the table in the centre of the room, Canela paused. 'You must take your book.' She picked it up and glanced at the details on the spine. 'Ah, yes. *Alice in Wonderland*. That lonely child, with her rabbit-holes and riddles and forlorn adventures.' She passed it to him. 'Some things are best forgotten. Or handed on.'

In the hall, as they moved towards the front door, Ian suddenly became aware of a commotion. A clattering and banging from behind the central staircase, in the vicinity of the lift.

'That wretched wheelchair!' Canela turned back and took a few steps towards the elevator. The metal gate was being opened to reveal an elderly fellow in slippers, trousers and a grey cardigan seated in the chair, hands on the big wheels, trying to edge it forward. Behind him, illuminated by the light bulb above her, Ingrid was leaning forward, doing what she could to assist the awkward departure.

'We will have to do something about this.' Canela, watching the struggle, had reverted to her frosty tone.

She turned to Ian. 'I spoke of art beginning with a glimpse of something. A human figure. A puzzling scene. Well, there's something puzzling for you. Right there, before you now, sits Marvic Blas Laredo. A spectral presence in what is written, but in the real world a driver with a different name, his true name, a man formerly employed by the Quirigo family. After that he became my loyal aide and eventually my friend.'

She smiled. 'He was handsome as Che in his youth. But unlike Che he wasn't venerated. He was knocked about in the back streets of the Witches' Market, simply because he resembled Che. He was bruised and injured badly. When I saw him struggling in later years, as he's struggling now, I suddenly pictured him as one of those who was with Che in a desolate ravine at the very end. I gave him that role in Laredo's writings. I let him escape with the others. Over the mountains to Santiago. A flight to the haven of Sydney Harbour. *Hay una Estrella*. I imagined a star. *La luna sobre el agua*. The moon over the water. A party and some local girls. Then a journey home.'

Her voice had dropped to a whisper, as if each word was strictly confidential. 'I gave him another name and a second life. Another existence. None of that means anything much to him, although it means much to me and others. I am fond of him. He was at my side years ago and he served me well. What he would like is a better wheelchair and a bigger TV set. He'll get them soon.'

There was nothing Ian could say about any of this, still not quite sure what to believe. Everything she said seemed deeply felt but, at the same time, fitted to the moment, as if her thoughts and the words she used were being constantly adjusted to suit her purposes. As the pushing and shoving was brought to an end and the wheelchair finally emerged from the lift, Canela greeted its appearance with a quiet smile and a look of amusement, as if both of its guardians, her old friend and her loyal niece, by their clumsy joint endeavours, had lifted her spirits and been restored to her deepest affection.

Ian's meeting with the lady had run its course. The wheelchair was now well and truly out of the lift. The elderly fellow was fumbling with the wheel brake. Ingrid had straightened up and was turning towards Ian, apprehensively, as if not quite sure what to make of his visit, and possibly wondering whether she had done the right thing in helping to bring it about. He acknowledged her presence, and what she had done for him, with a tiny bow, then moved towards the door.

He had met, at last, Canela Dochera. He had even managed to arrive at an understanding of sorts with the ingenious lady. He would have much to say in reporting back to his sister, but since much of what he needed to say would not be welcome, careful thought was required as to how the full story should be placed before her.

The best course might be to set out exactly what had happened and what had been said, without dissembling. As if he were simply recording events in a diary. A summary in that form might initially be greeted with consternation but it might well be enough in the end. Enough to convince Anita, once she had settled down, that he had done as much as he could for her. That there was no point in pushing ahead with her project, not along the lines she was suggesting. Marvic Blas Laredo was a will-o'-the-wisp in a tale going nowhere. A phantom at the far end of a library haunted by neglected books and the ghostly figures to be found within their pages.

The maid was standing at the front door, holding it open. She closed it softly behind him as he made his way out of the building.

The scene in the street below the front steps was much as he had left it. Where the clearing-out operation had started, two small tables and a high stool had been added to the fallen chair. Some distance away, brush in hand, the man with the step-ladder was studying the hoarding above him, staring upwards, as if still trying to work out what words or images should be set adrift in the blank space enclosed by its wooden frame.

Ian was about to walk away when he noticed that a sheet of paper had been slipped into the back of the Lewis Carroll book. Was it anything of importance? A letter belonging to a member of the household perhaps? Not sure what to do with it, but just in case it obliged him to return the gift, he unfolded the piece of paper. It proved to be a sheet with a handwritten poem upon it, lines scrawled beneath the title: *Canela in Wonderland.*

The raven and the writing desk.
Indeed, a fine riddle.

Think on it.

The black raven
and the wooden desk.
Here, the sombre bird.
The desk on the other hand.

Who can unravel
love's dark language –
Mad Hatter or March Hare?

Weeping in the hall,
older than a lifetime now,
she will never grow younger.
Love is mushroom-handed.
She will drown in her tears.

Open the desk.
Send forth thy raven.

The ark is a crumpled toy,
the world only
a rainbow bubble
floating away from the lips

of a lonely child
into space

into the rabbit-hole.

13

ANITA'S VERSION

I know what you're up to, Ian, and I don't like it. Not one little bit. It's apparent from your recent emails you've gone over to the dark side, encouraged by your friend the Maestro, no doubt. You're trying to talk me out of my project. Banging on about this or that, with the lofty voice people like you from Harvard or wherever always use. Banging on about being reasonable and so on, just to get your own way.

And now, in your latest effort, you want to make me believe that you've found your way to Canela Dochera. Amazing! I'm supposed to swallow everything she told you then about Marvic Laredo and his role in Che's final campaign. That, of course, will ruin my project. It won't work, Ian. Kim is beside me now, as I write this. She knows how to help me. Don't forget she's been a part-time lecturer in creative writing. So she can easily deconstruct your texts and little games, especially your latest fantasy.

First up, let me tell you this. Kim has been online for many hours of late over the past days. You won't be pleased to learn that in the course of her research she has tracked down an article by Kurt Meissner – Truth in Fiction – first published some years ago in an obscure Berlin journal called Am Rande de Nacht. *It was republished later by some friend of his in Havana, at greater length – but without getting any better.*

Your colleague Meissner, alias the Maestro, says, misleadingly in Kim's opinion, that the truth can sometimes only be told via a work of fiction. Which is what you are trying to do, raving on about books and riddles while cobbling together an account of your so-called visit to Canela Dochera. You finish up by claiming that Laredo never served with Che in any real sense. Preposterous! You say Dochera told you Laredo's writings are simply fabrications, tall stories written to protect her and her friends. Are you really asking us to believe that Dochera made up Marvic Blas Laredo? LOL!

Your whole account of your so-called visit is designed to send us off on a false trail. The red-herring roundabout, as Kim puts it. You give yourself away so obviously, and in so many ways, that we can scarcely believe you thought you could pull the wool over our eyes. But Kim knows the score. She once enrolled for a course about that sort of thing. Every writer is drawn towards the use of particular words and images, phrases revealing their mind-set and obsessions. These fingerprints are left behind in most of what they write, even when a nom de plume is being used. They give the game away. They can be used against the trickster as evidence of authorship.

This is certainly true of writers in the post-modern era – especially suckers for magic realism in the South American style. Scholarly tomes that don't exist. Libraries housing more books than were ever written. Maps the same size as the country they depict. Ends to never-ending stories that were meant to go on forever. Fables vindicating the actions of every person in the universe. There are always tell-tale habits. People who play far-fetched verbal games can't resist the temptation to leave clues and teasers along the way. Borges and his lot like to give people like themselves, supposedly ingenious literati, a chance of deciphering the coded meanings.

Put shortly, they want to have it both ways. They begin by writing in a style that will accomplish their hidden purpose, such as fabricating a diary or hiding behind a nom de plume, or coming up with a fake identity in order to rally readers to their cause. On the other hand, in the grip of an irresistible vanity, tricksters of this kind also want certain readers, of a discerning cast of mind – or so they presume – *to admire their skill in creating an entirely plausible account, albeit false, of what actually happened.*

This emerges from your friend the Maestro's article on truth in fiction. It's just another way of exercising power, a form of control, a means of making figures on the dance floor swirl around to a would-be Master's tune. Back and forth they go on the red-herring roundabout. It's all crap. In the course of her work in various institutions over the years – at tertiary level, she reminds me – Kim has become well-versed in the ins and outs of this deceitful process. She's been forced to call it out on a number of occasions, even at the expense of her own career, the promotions she might otherwise have obtained. A person of her calibre knows exactly what to look for and what to keep hidden.

It's not surprising, then, with all of this in her background, that she has drawn my attention to various tricks and feints that are visible in your email about the Dochera visit. Your pathetic attempt to talk me out of what I know I have to do. Let me walk you through some of the points she has made in the course of decoding what you've written, the vital points, the give-aways in both your last and earlier emails. As Kim puts it, the results are 'illuminating'.

A few examples. In an email you sent soon after my visit to Bolivia a year ago, you spoke of visiting Tarija with the Maestro. You said you were there to look at various artefacts and records relevant to your work at the Chiquitos missions. You said these were held by a local museum. You mentioned your surprise in finding that many of the Jesuit books and ledgers dating back to the 16th and 17th centuries were simply heaped up in unsorted stacks in a back room of the museum. Clearly at risk, according to you, of being lost or mislaid, because none of the local people seemed to know much about them. I still have the photo that came with your email, showing old cardboard boxes marked 1719-22 and 1669-74, and so on, going right back.

According to you, while staring at the jumbled heaps, the Maestro said: 'This comes from the imperfect past, but we could be looking at the *imperfections of a world to come.'* This is very close to a phrase you attribute to Canela while looking at a shelf of classic books in her library.

You may try to explain away this sort of thing by calling it mere coincidence. Fat chance. It is clear to us, being well and truly alert to the way such mannerisms appear in written works, your account of what took place in the Dochera household can't be trusted. This is obvious also from the various literary allusions scattered through the story in your last email, your little box of tricks and riddles.

On your way to Canela's house, for instance, you picture an Aymaran woman boarding a bus. There she is on her journey home with a black bird in a wire cage. A silhouette with folded wings. Such an obvious link to Kafka's single-sentence fable about domestic oppression: A cage went in search of a bird.

You present a picture of hammers on a door-knocker to the Dochera premises. Far from these fulfilling a pure, symbolic function, you describe them being put to 'practical use' as the visitor supposedly knocks on the front door to gain admittance. In this way you none-too-subtly mock the use of tropes and symbols in literary works.

You speak implausibly of being given a book about Alice in Wonderland. You finish up quoting a poem supposedly left in the book, based on some of Alice's adventures in the rabbit-hole. You mention Goya's Sleep of Reason. You speak of 'cryptic messages.' You mention a lift going nowhere in a lift shaft. You describe a sign-writer in Canela's street staring at a blank hoarding, not knowing what to say. All of this leaves an impression (with a wink and a nudge to a 'discerning' reader) that your alleged account of what Canela said emerges from a black hole in space, and will soon be drawn back to where it came from when the game is over, a place from which no light escapes.

Fabrications and embellishments of this kind are not only unbelievable but so obvious. According to Kim this is a classic case of the ingenious trickster (in this case not so ingenious) seeking to win approval for his lies by planting clues and pointing to what he thinks will be admired as his extraordinary skill.

It pains me deeply to say it, but we simply do not believe that you ever managed to speak to Canela Dochera. We don't believe that she portrayed Laredo as a figment of her imagination, just a will-o'-the-wisp.

We're conscious also that even if you did contrive some kind of meeting with the lady, no weight can be attached to anything she might have told you. Why so? Because a skilled falsifier of reality, as everyone seems to think she is, would be quite capable of making up a plausible story to lay before you, a story with all the twists and turns you've laid before us: writings supposedly created to disguise the betrayals behind Che's downfall; the casting of doubt on his heroic status; ambiguities concerning his death and burial, and so on. For that very reason, we are inclined to believe that Canela Dochera probably did persuade some special friend of hers to pose as a museum curator in Havana, and to send us the pieces supposedly written by Laredo that got me started. Nothing else rings true.

Whichever way we look at it, nothing useful has come out of your enquiries in La Paz. How ineffectual you are! Maybe you were trying to be fair. Maybe you've been acting as you thought was best – as you often mistakenly do – albeit led astray by others along the way.

In the end, however, whether or not you actually met Canela Dochera may not matter. We've been making our own enquiries, joining the dots. The chaotic events surrounding Che's final hours after the ambush at La Higuera seem to have left things up in the air. Created a vacuum. The confusion at Vallegrande around the laying-out of what was thought to be his body has added to the likelihood that he managed to outwit his captors. Our recent research shows, quite clearly, that there were insiders among the people coming and going at the Vallegrande hospital. People sympathetic to Che's cause, who were quite capable of substituting one body for another.

The absence of a verified corpse, plus misleading talk about a supposed cremation, which is now known not to have taken place, adds extra weight to this conclusion. This is why informed commentators have always asked: why did the Bolivian high command claim Che was cremated, but later come up with a story that their famous captive was one of the fallen rebels buried in a grave adjacent to an airstrip on the outskirts of Vallegrande? Quite clearly, because they had something to hide. One smokescreen after another. You'll recall the article I mentioned in one of my earlier emails by the Spanish journalists Bertrand de la Grange and Maite Rico. They make the case that the bones at Vallegrande, which were supposedly identified as Che's remains in order to facilitate a triumphant reburial in Cuba 30 years after his death, were not in fact his remains.

More importantly, after talking to some of those who were at the party in Sydney held for survivors of the Bolivian campaign, it seems that one member of the group closely resembled Che. This may have been Laredo, because he's said to have looked somewhat like his leader. But when one fits the various pieces of the jigsaw together, there's a real likelihood that the body brought by helicopter from the schoolhouse at La Higuera to the hospital room at Vallegrande, which was then identified as Che by a CIA agent, was actually that of Laredo. Che escaped, and for some years after his return to Cuba led a hidden life, cloaked by anonymity to avert the risk of assassination.

There is support for all of this in our mother's autobiography. The manuscript is patchy, as you're well aware, but I feel sure you will agree she gives a reasonably detailed account of her work with the Liberation News Service in New York.

When she speaks of the South American journalist who befriended her at that time, the man in question seems to have known a good deal about the Cuban revolution and Fidel Castro's personal habits – almost as if, like Che, he had fought at Castro's side. Her reference to being close to this man in the vicinity of a bridge, as if they had met before, at a party in Sydney perhaps, is significant too.

We're pursuing some further leads at the moment, before reaching any final conclusion as to the journalist's true identity. But we have reason to believe from some of the enquiries we've already made, and from what we've found online about the Kennedy assassination, that the journalist we thought was Laredo, but now believe was actually Che, probably ended up being gunned down by anti-Castro Cubans in Miami, soon after leaving New York.

You'll see immediately the importance of these enquiries. We thought Laredo important enough to become a sculpted image above the entrance to the Art Gallery of New South Wales. We have to accept, however, irrespective of the doubts we have about your alleged meeting with Canela Dochera, that Laredo isn't widely enough known. It would be comparatively easy for bourgeois opinion to denigrate his role in joining Che's forces to create a revolution and a new society. It's easy also to question his links to the Australian settlement in Paraguay, as you've done, and to doubt his true identity. But Che is a bigger fish to fry.

If it turns out that Che came to Australia in the aftermath of his magnificent campaign, his attempt to set up a truly enlightened state in South America, then my entry for the art competition must be reconfigured. Che is obviously much bigger than all this and his reputation among progressive thinkers is unassailable. No one would dare question the suitability of the sculpted image we now have in mind: Che's resolute gaze and dark beret, the face of a new society.

If you can find anything that might be of use to us in this before leaving La Paz, it would be greatly appreciated by your sister. The deadline for my entry is fast approaching. I will wait to hear from you as soon as possible. You can see from what I've said that I have good reason to believe that my version of the truth is closer to what has to be done than any other. More importantly perhaps, in the life of a practising artist who seeks to explain a nation to itself, my reality is the one that counts. Entonces, as you say in Bolivia. So there you have it. Anita.

14

ENDGAME

The straight-backed wooden chairs in the waiting room at the Concepción courthouse must have been fashioned to suit what Ian was beginning to think was their real purpose: causing discomfort, as a warning to litigants or witnesses waiting their turn to enter the adjoining courtroom. A way of punishing them a little, before they were sworn in and proceeded to unburden themselves by telling their stories. A signal perhaps that perjurers could be exposed to even greater discomfort, a dire penalty, if they failed to speak truly.

The delay. The hard wooden seat. Ian rose to his feet and massaged his backside, as he had done several times already. He flexed his legs. He had agreed to accompany the Maestro to the local courthouse where his colleague was to speak for one of their workers, a member of the digging team who had been charged with theft, the removal of a bag of tools from an excavation behind the mission church.

The Maestro's role was to say the worker was a man of good character. The removal was due to a misunderstanding. The Maestro seemed to think that his testimony would only take a few minutes. In any event, it might be useful for Ian to come along in case he too was needed as a witness.

Ian had been in La Paz, attending to his sister's requirements, when the bag of tools disappeared from the site. He could add nothing much to the Maestro's evidence concerning the alleged theft, but he was willing to do what he could to vouch for the man's good character. Besides, the walk to the courthouse was an opportunity for him to update the Maestro about Anita's project and the outcome of his inquiries in La Paz.

He had covered as much as possible on their way to the court, but it was only a short walk and much remained to be said. Upon arrival, however, the local *abogado* – the lawyer involved in the case – had immediately hurried the Maestro into the courtroom right away, telling Ian to stay in the waiting room.

The Maestro's testimony certainly seemed to be taking longer than expected. To flex the legs and massage the backside wasn't quite enough. So Ian strolled to the far end of the room for a look at the notice-board fixed to a side wall beneath the court's crest. It displayed a batch of official notices, the court list, alongside pamphlets mentioning local attractions.

There were people on chairs at this end of the room. A woman in an embroidered cloak. She was holding the hand of a teenage Guarani boy with a dazed look on his face. Another woman, close by, was leaning forward intently, doing her best to catch whatever advice she was receiving from her well-groomed lawyer.

A few minutes ago, after entering the waiting room with his client, this lawyer had looked around and, upon noticing Ian, had immediately dug into the pocket of his jacket. With a broad smile, he had crossed the room to hand over his business card. He was offering Ian another smile now, as if to confirm that his initial approach was simply the first step in what might prove to be a close relationship. Ian answered the *abogado*'s latest and even more effusive smile with a tiny bow and turned back to the notice-board.

There were various cases on the court list, with the Maestro's case somewhere in the middle. The other sheets of paper were mostly police and governmental messages about missing persons and travel restrictions in the region. The pamphlets singled out various attractions that were likely to be of interest to visitors, such as the Artisan Workshops and the Gran Hotel with its famous collection of indigenous masks. Inevitably, the largest and most colourful pamphlet drew attention to the world heritage cultural sites in the area: *Patrimonio Cultural de la Humanidad: Missions Jesuiticas*. These were named after the early Jesuit settlements. The magnificent cathedral at Concepción was described as still in the course of being restored by European experts. There was a picture also of the bell-tower outside the cathedral. This was accompanied by a glimpse of the adjoining cloisters.

Ian glanced at his watch and returned to his seat.

In the absence of anything else to read he felt in his pocket to find the lawyer's business card. The heading, *Abogado*, was positioned above a familiar image of the blindfolded female justice figure, a sword in one hand, uplifted scales of justice in the other. As to *Procesos*, the services available to clients covered a broad and disturbing range of possibilities: *penales, policiales, accidents de tránsito, narcóticos*. Beneath the list the designer of the card had added what seemed to be a final optimistic flourish – *Abogado de los Casos Imposible* – as if, even in a mundane court of law, impossible cases could still miraculously be won with the help of an ingenious lawyer.

He pocketed the card. Findings in a court of law or in a work of history based on verifiable facts were familiar forms of truth. But the Maestro, in his article published in Berlin and later in Havana, had argued that certain truths could only be brought to light and conveyed persuasively by works of fiction. Controversial truths, for example, or matters that in puritanical times people feel they can't talk about,

The Maestro had gone on to say, with respect to works of fiction about puzzling events, that the way the story ended might turn out to be less interesting than the quest for the truth, the attempt to fathom underlying realities. Don Quixote's misadventures, for example, a tale having more to do with the hero's unsettled state of mind than with the way people actually behave in facing challenges, could be the source of unexpected truths about human behaviour. This might even turn out to be one of the crucial truths behind some matter at the heart of a tale, or even the only truth available.

Perhaps it was only by thinking in this wide-ranging way that the complexity of a complex situation could be fully revealed. Assertions in history books, or findings made by a court of law, even after a careful selection of what were thought to be the vital facts, might simply finish up reducing what everyone thought was an open-and-shut case to something less than that, a mere glimpse of the entire tangled picture.

In the course of his email exchanges with Anita, Ian had tried to remind her of the visit they had made together to the Art Gallery of New South Wales, followed by their short walk beneath the Moreton Bay fig trees on the edge of the Domain: to show her the 'Mosman stone' and explain its link to the Thornton family.

His aim had been to edge her away from disappearing into a rabbit-hole of unreality, a dark pit concerning the life and times of a South American revolutionary called Marvic Blas Laredo.

To Anita and her friends, artists and others in contemporary times were to be judged essentially by their identities, and that depended not on individual skills and achievements but on the nature of the group the person was associated with. If this group or cohort could claim to have been treated badly, denied privileges vested in others, so much the better.

This unwavering kind of thought had no doubt led to Anita and her friend Kim refusing to believe Ian's account of his visit to Canela Dochera's household. And now, they had adopted an even bolder position, a reconfiguration of the facts gathered in the course of their so-called 'further research'. They had arrived at a tentative but exciting belief of their own. It was clearly a deeply-rooted feeling, very close to a certainty: Che had survived his 'final' campaign.

Ian could scarcely bring himself to repeat to the Maestro all that had been covered in Anita's latest email. To describe her claims aloud, even in the presence of the Maestro, a scholar accustomed to dealing with whatever peculiarities the world threw at him, from dinosaur prints in former mudflats to ornate rock carvings in desolate places, it was so embarrassing. No one cares about the facts these days seemed to be the view underlying Anita's increasingly ambitious narrative. To her and Kim, the important thing in establishing truths that really mattered was to set out what a person with a conscience ought to believe, and the best way of making other people believe it too.

Still lost in his thoughts, it took Ian a moment to realise that the door marked Tribunal de Sentencia had just been opened. A uniformed official emerged, followed by the Maestro. His ordeal over, presumably, his testimony delivered, Ian's mentor seemed to be in a fine mood as he approached. 'All done!' he announced. 'No need for you to be called. I think we'll get the result we wanted.'

He waited patiently as Ian rose to his feet. They headed for the door leading to the veranda which provided a fine view of the bell-tower and stately cathedral on the far side of the square.

'Now then,' the Maestro said briskly. 'You were telling me about your sister's latest move.'

'I'm having trouble putting her latest position succinctly. The whole thing seems so bizarre.'

'Weird?'

'Or even worse.'

'You told me about her email casting doubts on your visit to Canela Dochera. Calling it fiction. Did she and her friend have anything to go on in that regard?'

'Nothing much. Anita drew attention to what were arguably flaws in my account of what happened. Canela's remarks about neglected classics in her library, for example, were said to be suspiciously close to what you once said about the old Jesuit records we saw in Tarija. Also tragically neglected. I quote both of you as saying that this could be a glimpse of the past or of a world to come.'

'I can't recall making a comment to that effect, but it's the sort of thing I might have said.'

'There's the point. Looking back at my notes, I can't quite recall what Canela is supposed to have said about those texts in her library. The words attributed to her may have contained an echo of what you said on an earlier occasion. Inadvertently, I may have jotted down something of that sort. I can't be sure. My fear is that a slip of any kind may have been just enough for Anita and her friend, in their highly suspicious state of mind, to doubt everything said about the visit.'

'The same thing happens with site reports and reviews of history books. People believe what they want to believe. Each generation pokes holes in the work of their predecessors.'

'There was little merit in her other criticisms. Enough to convince literary critics, perhaps, but not a court of law. So I feel safe in standing by my report to Anita.'

'If this were politics, an admission on TV of some minor slip would be enough to hang you.'

'This *is* politics. And my slip is not the worst of it. Anita and her friend felt I hadn't answered their criticisms. So they decided to chart their own course. I don't know exactly what their further research consists of, but they now seem quite convinced that Canela orchestrated everything that has come to light, from conspiring with the museum curator in Havana – the person who initially posted Laredo's writings to Anita – to fabricating accounts of what happened to Che at La Higuera and Vallegrande.'

'Why would Canela do that?'

'To conceal matters that might tarnish Che's reputation.'

'But it seems from the description of your visit to Canela's household, and of her admission that she and others turned against Che, that the lady did finish up doubting Che's achievements.'

'Indeed. Hence the need to invent Laredo and an article by him portraying Che's Bolivian campaign in a positive way. In concealing matters that might tarnish Che's reputation, and the reputation of those around him, Canela is seeking to conceal the role she and her group played in Che's downfall.'

'But your sister doesn't believe any of this.'

'Apparently not. Now that they have done some further research.'

'What *do* they believe?'

Ian took a deep breath. 'I can scarcely bring myself to say it.'

'Say it.'

'They now believe that in the confusion surrounding the final battle at La Higuera, and the supposed identification and cremation of Che's body at Vallegrande, Che escaped. Marvic Laredo, a man who resembled the guerrilla leader, was the man captured and disposed of. Che joined the group of survivors who spent a few days in Sydney on their way back to Cuba, which is where he probably met and maybe had a fling with Anita's mother, Lucy Thornton.'

'Amazing!' A bewildered gesture underlined the Maestro's exclamation. 'Like a bolt from the blue! Where does all of this come from?'

'They seem to have pieced all this together from various so-called reliable sources. Their belief is that Che's allies in Cuba and La Paz, including the skilful Canela, or someone like her, were well-aware that news of Che's survival and escape could never be revealed. Otherwise he would be immediately assassinated, if not by the CIA – whose reputation was on the line as the party that verified his death – then by the military leaders in La Paz. After all, it was they who claimed credit for having disposed of the notorious Che Guevara. And there were others, of course. Those who had been opposed to Che's Bolivian campaign from the outset. Agents of Moscow on the left, and various anti-Castro activists on the right.'

Ian paused to let this sink in before continuing. 'According to Anita and her friend, the Laredo story wasn't created in order to cover up the betrayals leading to Che's downfall, as I was told by Canela. It was created to cover up Che's escape from southern Bolivia via Santiago and Sydney, and his inglorious death some years later.'

'What exactly do you mean by that?'

'I mean nothing by it. I'm simply trying to pass on what my sister and her friend have come to believe.'

'Which is?'

'That after escaping from Vallegrande, and returning to Cuba via Sydney, Che lived anonymously to avoid assassination, posing as a journalist. In that role, some years later, he visited the Liberation News Service in New York, which led to a reunion with Lucy Thornton. On the way back to Havana, however, the indications are that he was gunned down ingloriously by certain anti-Castro Cubans in Miami. Anita and her friend have yet to verify the facts underlying their so-called research – but seem to think they can do so.'

'I have to sit.' The Maestro, breathing heavily, led the way to a bench beneath a ragged palm tree. 'So fascinating. But what's the point of it all? Why are your sister and her friend cobbling all of this together?'

'For the art project.'

'How so? I thought they'd given up on the Laredo thing?'

'Not entirely. At one stage they harboured a belief that Anita's mother may have had an affair with Laredo. That Anita may have been Laredo's love child. But now, having formed a view that Laredo was the man buried at Vallegrande, they seem to think that Che may be Anita's father.'

'You'll have to take me through this slowly.' The Maestro raised a hand to his chest. 'I'm still trying to take it all in.'

'If indeed Che assumed Laredo's identity,' Ian went on, 'and escaped to Sydney with Pombo and the other survivors, then various other things fall into place, according to Anita and her friend. After finding his way back to Cuba, Che posed as a journalist to hide his true identity. His trip to New York in that role led not just to a reunion with Lucy Thornton, but to a passionate affair. It seems likely, according to Kim Guest, that Anita, via her mother, is the product of that brief but memorable liaison. If indeed Che was gunned down soon after leaving New York, then his consummation of the affair with Anita's mother was probably his last sexual fling. His last embrace.'

'But what good would that be to Anita and her friend, even it be true?'

'The truth, as we used to speak of it, may not matter much any more. These days, it seems, in the new world of contemporary art and thought, you can be whoever you want to be. Their notion is that it will improve Anita's prospects in the Art Gallery competition. If she can establish a paternal link to Che, her identity will be that of an artist linked to a victim of colonial oppression who became a famous freedom fighter. She would be acclaimed as the product of Che's historic last embrace, a daughter endowed with all his qualities by descent: a victim with vast iconic media power. A perfect end to a fine tale.'

Ian sighed, having managed, somehow, to unfold the latest twist in what seemed to be a never-ending story. 'So there it is. A sculpted image of Che placed above the entrance to the Art Gallery of New South Wales, the work of an artist who is also his daughter. If the artist is able to confirm that the legendary hero set foot on Australian soil in the aftermath of a splendid campaign in South America, then that would reinforce the perfect outcome. Che's image above the entrance would be a magnificent assertion of what the world could and should be. Their belief was, of course, that in this fully-awakened day and age the hero, the subject of the image, and the iconic image itself, are so revered by cultural leaders that no one would dare criticise the trustees for exhibiting the profile so prominently.'

'And has this strategy worked? Where has it all finished up?'

Ian joined his friend and mentor on the bench, sitting down slowly and carefully, still shaken by everything he had felt obliged to say, and still had to say in order to complete the bewildering story. 'Their strategy might have worked, if the new plan had been executed smoothly. But it wasn't. I gather from the email I received this morning that Anita and her friends in the collective got so excited by the possibilities of their research that they lost sight of the deadline for the entry. They've never been good at attending to details like that. They ran out of time. Anita's submission fell by the wayside. Her entry was never put in. So we'll never know what the trustees might have done with it.'

'All your hard work for nothing.'

Ian raised his eyes to the old but beautifully-restored cathedral at the far side of the square, a fine creation brought back from its ruined state. 'One never knows what the future holds,' he murmured. 'History is what it is, and artists are what they are.'

The Maestro smiled. He waved a hand at their surroundings: the palm trees on the fringes of the square, the dirt path leading to the bell-tower and the majestic cathedral behind it. 'Here, in the presence of palm trees and historic structures, I am beginning to enjoy this latest twist in the narrative. And I'm wondering where it will end. Or whether the end will prove to be constantly elusive, as in most tales conveyed by words and images, including revered chronicles. Nonetheless, if the ingenious Canela, or someone like her, is behind it all, then the search for meaning must begin with the writings we have. Right back to Laredo's article. We must ponder what was said or left unsaid.'

He let his hand drift outwards again. 'Our surroundings remind me, of course, that we are close to what was once the outermost limits of the Incan empire, a regime held together by cities, roads and frontier forts but having no form of writing.'

'We understand from Laredo's article,' he continued, 'and indeed from the diaries of others, that towards the end of the Bolivian campaign, Che raided Samaipata, principally to obtain medical supplies to treat his asthma. Could it be, that the author of Laredo's writings may also have been drawing our attention to something else? At Samaipata, as you are well aware, one finds the massive rock formation, inscribed with mystical symbols, known as El Fuerte. This fortress, at the far end of the empire, was a place where countless tales of war and peace must have been told. But in the absence of Incan records, apart from *quipus*, the knots they tied in strings to record transactions, the nature of such tales remains a mystery.

'Yes, our judgement of what happened in that place in Incan times, the meaning of that facet of their past, is left in mid-air, open to a variety of suppositions and interpretations. One begins to wonder whether this is what lay behind the Incan disregard of written records. In the absence of a lasting record the meaning of the past is always in the hands of the living. They can bring the past to fruition in whatever way they wish. And thus more easily control the present and the future. The same might be said of those among our colleagues, as I once reminded you, for whom phantoms of the present – the things they want now – so often haunt their renditions of the past. As if pointing the way to what they hope will be a better world, a realm reflecting their own dreams and values and beliefs. They attach their site reports and articles to generally-approved strings of information. But as we used to say at Café Tortoni: life is never what we write, and there is always more to be said on both sides of every story.'

'So where are all these thoughts leading?' Seated beside the Maestro,

Ian felt obliged to pin down his companion. 'For myself, I can't see any enjoyment in what you call this latest twist in my sister's tale. If everything is left up in the air as to what things mean, then we will soon be left with nothing. An absence of knowledge will lead to an absence of commonly-accepted facts and social values, a lack of any demonstrable reality. It will then become impossible to persuade people from one position to another, or of the need to pursue a constructive course. People will become accustomed to believing random facts in setting out their values. Their version of reality will be a heap of fragments. Bits and pieces from online, reflecting confusion. As Anita and her friends seem willing to accept already.'

The Maestro nodded. He was sitting comfortably, hands clasped across his paunch. 'That's my point. Anita and her friends, consciously or sub-consciously, may have found their way to something of significance. These days, frenetically, the internet and its related twitterings take us everywhere, and to all the problems to be found in unfamiliar corners of the world, until the only way to survive is by inattention, or by finding solace in the art or music of such places.'

He felt obliged to elaborate. 'Artists have always been in the business of responding to what goes on around them. Rulers and their subjects in other eras were usually lucid, aiming for coherence in the way they managed their affairs, even in chaotic times. This was reflected in their literature and works of art. But now, with constant obfuscation in political discourse, rants and rambling on social media, language has ceased to be a medium of truth or persuasive meaning. Not surprisingly, then, obscurity in art has become a familiar strategy. Whatever you can get away with. In the new reality, everything is malleable, even facts and figures. The challenge for a contemporary artist is to provide a compelling representation of the void, the dark hole into which things that used to be worth saying or conserving gradually disappear.'

The Maestro spread his hands. 'The only way of providing such a picture, a representation of this important truth, is to proceed equivocally, by the use of subterfuge and fictions, as I mentioned when I met you for lunch at the Varino courtyard. If your sister claims to be the product of Che's last embrace, she is simply responding to the chaotic patterning of the times, as an artist should. *Well done*, it might be said. *Keep going*. Which eventually might add some further twists to the tale.'

Ian turned to face him. 'Are you seriously suggesting, in answering my sister's latest email, that I should praise her insight and creative skill?'

'You can do so if you wish.'

'I can now see why you're enthralled by all of this. It's the same as Canela enjoying creating Marvic Blas Laredo and fabricating his memoir. It resonates with the article you published about the presence of truth in fiction.' He paused. 'Unless, of course, it wasn't Canela but someone else who created Laredo.'

The Maestro seemed amused by this further notion. 'Some other person on the way to some other world!'

His ironic tone made Ian pause again. 'Or maybe some other person who created Canela Dochera,' he added, speaking carefully. 'If one covers all the possibilities.'

'Or gave Canela certain lines to say in playing her part?'

The Maestro seemed to be enjoying himself, as if a new line of thought was always worth pursuing. This often happened in his daily work, as Ian was well aware, when a trench collapsed or the strategy behind an excavation had to be re-examined. But today was different. There was an eagerness in his manner which reminded Ian that in addition to his expertise as an archaeologist the Maestro was known for admiring myths and imaginary tales, partly because, in certain cultural settings, they were a way of exploring controversial events. Discussion about what they meant could run in various directions without restraint.

Ian studied the Maestro thoughtfully, wondering what to say next. He was also reminded by their discussion that the Maestro had colleagues in Cuba. His Berlin article had been republished by a friend in Havana. In addition to writers and editors in that city, he would certainly know a number of museum curators.

'Instead of creating Canela,' Ian inquired, 'or giving her useful lines to say, could some other person have acted as her so-called 'special friend' in Havana? Or posed as such while living somewhere else?'

The elderly scholar smiled. 'Perhaps or perhaps not. Who could be sure, with all this talk of fantasy and fiction in the air. Fiction is what it might or might not be.'

He sat up straight, getting ready to depart. 'Which means, like the so-called truth of a matter, we may never know what the story really is or where it will end. Which could be useful. Imagination fosters memory. So much in a person's past is infused with self-deception. But recollections of luminous moments that we can't forget are tied to deeper feelings, and leave us dreaming of what could be our better selves.'

The Maestro took a deep breath and slowly rose to his feet. 'Let us leave this weird bench where I had to sit and resume our walk.'

He paused to hitch up his trousers, glancing at the green fronds above them as he did so, and at the patch of shade they were leaving. 'When one knows the truth,' he declared in a formal tone, as if to bring the discussion to an end, 'it can often be useful to save the knowledge one has for some other occasion. To speak not of what one knows but of palm trees and their tantalising fronds. In the hope that what they leave dangling in the air will not only cast a calming spell but always be with us.'

Ian wasn't sure what lay behind these words, or what they might reveal about steps taken by his colleague to assist Canela.

Then, for some reason he couldn't quite explain, and would have difficulty explaining to those around him in times to come when talking about his years with the Maestro, he glanced at the bench they had just vacated and at the tall, impassive palm tree nearby.

The words used by Javier Facundas in La Paz, had suddenly come to mind. *Where the Maestro sits in all of this is a tale for another day.*

A few days after these words had been uttered, Ian recalled, he and the Maestro had sat at a marble-topped table in the Varino courtyard, sipping wine. They had watched the elderly musicians on their makeshift bandstand present a suite of tango tunes to the people brought to their feet by the beguiling music, various couples under the coloured baubles of light, dancing briskly to and fro in their customary manner, like marionettes on a brightly-lit stage.

'The play's the thing,' the Maestro had observed while he sat there, calmly and patiently, enjoying the tango rhythms and theatrical scene before him. He had spoken quietly, but intensely, with an air of expectancy, as if looking forward to the day when any strings controlling the twists and turns of the figures on the dance floor would be cast off, as if hoping that stories about luminous moments of this kind, the dreams reflected in the dancers' intricate steps and firm but fleeting embraces, would be fully understood and never forgotten. The way of life and the freedom behind the music becoming theirs forever.

Milton Keynes UK
Ingram Content Group UK Ltd.
UKHW011834090124
435754UK00004B/315